THE SWEET CHEAT GONE

Gregor Roy MacGregor, young Scottish artist commissioned to paint a mural for Rowe's mega business combine, meets and marries their heiress. Or does he? In the tragic events that swiftly follow, he finds himself fighting to prove his sanity and his innocence. Following doggedly a few apparently meaningless clues into a dangerous vortex of vice, murder and mayhem, he takes on singlehanded the whole compulsive might of Rowe's empire. Even his own brother and Eva who loves him, turn against him. His life constantly threatened in a race against time, flight from Rowe's Vale takes him to the Highlands and back to an asylum for the insane, his only friend a helpless old man from an abandoned village about to be lost forever under the growing town's new reservoir. There in a chilling denouement, at the mercy of ruthless killers, the truth – and death – await obliteration by the released flood waters.

Books should be returned on or before the
last date stamped below.

NORTH EAST of SCOTLAND LIBRARY SERVICE
MELDRUM MEG WAY, OLDMELDRUM

THE SWEET CHEAT GONE

A Crime Novel

by

ALANNA KNIGHT

MyS
432220

This first world edition published in Great Britain 1992 by
SEVERN HOUSE PUBLISHERS LTD of
35 Manor Road, Wallington, Surrey SM6 0BW
First published in the U.S.A. 1992 by
SEVERN HOUSE PUBLISHERS INC of
475 Fifth Avenue, New York, NY 10017.

British Library Cataloguing in Publication Data
Knight, Alanna
   Sweet Cheat Gone.
   I. Title
   813.914 [F]

   ISBN 0-7278-4379-6

Printed and bound in Great Britain by Dotesios Limited,
Trowbridge, Wiltshire

For Alistair

. . . Silence. Still faint on the porch
  Brake the flames of the stars.
In gloom gropes a hope-wearied hand
  Over keys, bolts, and bars.
A face peered. All the grey night
  In chaos of vacancy shone;
Nought but vast sorrow was there –
  The sweet cheat gone.

(From: THE GHOST by Walter de la Mare.)

PART ONE

OPHELIA: 'Tis brief, my lord.
HAMLET: As woman's love
(Shakespeare)

CHAPTER ONE

Anger. Blazing, white-hot, blinding anger. With the rain leaking down my coat-collar; with the stubborn-faced girl who stared defiantly up at me, raindrops turning her blonde hair into unreconisable elf-locks. Anger with destiny and its jaundiced sense of humour, bringing the miracle of this girl for a few weeks, then tearing us apart.

For this undoubtedly was the final parting. Time was no longer measurable in days, only seconds remained.

I tried once more. Banal words, repeated so often that they had acquired a sheep-like quality, the vain, poor bleating of an animal in torment. "But why not, Laurel, why not? Come with me. Please! I love you, I need you. What's changed you? What have I done? Tell me, tell me!"

Furiously watching her give an ineffectual tug at the lurid headscarf, caring more about protecting her hair than answering. "I don't know, Greg. I'm sorry. I just don't love you, that's all." And in that couldn't-care-less shrug, all kindness, all pretence were gone. She was bored and tired and wanted done with it. She looked up slowly. "If you want the truth – I never did love you."

Never! All the love, all the vows crumbled into ridicule and hypocrisy, the joy and the ecstacy cancelled out by three words. "I never did."

The anger hitherto controlled, exploded inside me. I must have hurt her arm, for she cried out, and a small crowd slowed down to watch something more interesting than the shop-windows' pre-Christmas display. There were nudges, sniggers, at this parade of our matrimonial difficulties.

Laurel stood rubbing her arm, watching me ruefully. Even physical violence could not stir her emotions, for her voice was flat and indifferent as she said: "I didn't mean to hurt you, Greg, but please, please go away from here. That's why I wanted to have lunch with you – the only reason. To tell you, but you won't listen." Urgency brought animation to her voice. "Go anywhere, but go quick. Get away from here."

"Why should I? Just to save your face and make things easier for you? To make all your lies sound more convincing, is that it?"

Biting her lip, she shook her head slowly, its silvery-blondeness unrecognisably dark in the rain. Perhaps with the illusion of love gone too, she looked older, harder, the blue eyes paler, calculating and cold. There was something less than perfection in the heavy layer of make-up, rain-streaked and messy, in what to my love-besotted eyes had appeared the pure radiance of unblemished youth.

"Things won't be easier for me, Greg. It's for you this time." She hesitated, looking swiftly over her shoulder. It was that odd indefinable gesture I had noticed at lunch, as though someone watched.

Maybe I imagined the fear in her eyes as she said hurriedly, "There could be danger, don't you understand? Danger for you."

I laughed. "Danger from Uncle Hartley or from Rowe's thugs, d'you mean? Danger at laying my dirty hands on their precious heiress?"

She looked bewildered and defeated, or maybe that was the rain too. "You won't listen, will you? You're so stubborn, so sure of yourself. All right, Greg. You may not get another chance, I'm only telling you this because you seem too nice – to get – to get mixed up in this kind of thing."

4

"Seem too nice, eh?" Another nail hammered into my wounded pride. Surely if you have loved and married someone, however briefly, it was an unnecessary observation that they "seemed nice."

"Go to hell!" And pushing her roughly aside, I ran across the busy road, cars hooting their angry disapproval at my heels. Perhaps the nightmare would have ended there, had I not looked back, expecting her to be gone.

She stood motionless, watching, head well down, peering into the rain. But neither distance nor rain concealed the naked anguish in her eyes. Anguish and that indefinable something else, to which I was still a stranger.

Furiously I started walking away. Her shout must have been good and loud to cut across the stream of traffic.

"Greg!"

And even as I turned, she was half-way across the road, head down after me, running blindly through the rain.

The driver of the car didn't have a chance, and even in that moment I felt a shaft of pity for the poor devil as the brakes screamed and she vanished beneath his wheels.

From then until the day when I realised how imperative it was to remember every single detail of that last meeting, my mind skated perilously on the outer edge of reality. Half insane with grief and remorse, dallying with small useless things, persuading the green-faced motorist and his sobbing wife, innocently embarked on an afternoon's shopping, that he could not be blamed. Both of us telling the policeman what had happened, wondering why Laurel lay so still, and where in God's name was the ambulance?

Dear faithful Eva was there for the kill, too. Hovering like an outsize cellophane parcel, in plastic raincoat and hat, clutching her enormous shopping basket of uncertain antiquity. She held Laurel's gloves and handbag and watched over us, clucking anxiously and treating me like a naughty child who has wilfully destroyed a precious toy.

5

Laurel's eyelids stirred. Her lips moved. "Quick . . ." she murmured.

"What is it, darling? You're going to be all right."

The words were lost, thick and incomprehensible, only one came through ". . . quick . . ."

Then her eyes glazed, and she smiled unseeingly, at a point beyond us. I didn't need Eva's hoarse whisper: "Who is Vic? It's Vic, she's asking for."

"Vic! . . . oh, Vic! . . ." Then with the ambulance racing down on us, she was dead. Her outstretched hand, her unseeing, imploring eyes searching for him, this unknown. This Vic, whom she had loved.

CHAPTER TWO

What happened afterwards is mercifully hazy, or perhaps a simple matter of mind retreating before enormity. All that remains are curious disjointed incidents, the compassion in strangers' eyes, watching the doctor's shiny bald head as he knelt in the rain: "I'm sorry, There's nothing we can do."

The dead face, no longer Laurel's, already changed, remote and inaccessible in death. Wishing as I knelt there, to crumble away, to be washed out, nullified by the late autumn rain.

The ambulance gone, I began walking.

After a while, I wasn't alone and desperate as the sorrow, was the desire to get rid of Eva. Big, tall Eva, my unofficial keeper, with her shopping basket bludgeoning the crowds and earning us nasty looks on buses. The "shopper" that never left her, day or night, never emptied, its gloomy depths the plethora of departed seasons, last year's Christmas card, broken sunglasses, patterns for garments never made.

With her free arm, she steered me through what remained of the day like a blind man's dog. At a time like that, sheer ingratitude seemed mean and contemptuous, like being embarrassed by the shopping basket, and across a cafe table, being fascinated by the black down on her upper lip, growing daily more like the beginnings of a fine military moustache.

As she paid for coffees, lit my cigarettes, and gloriously took charge of the situation, the picture that was building up was frightening enough. With her sole rival, Laurel, gone, she was going to relish every moment of sticking my shattered remains, like a protesting, unwilling Humpty Dumpty, together again.

Our route homeward to my lodgings included several bars where, hell-bent on detachment, I sought refuge in the oblivion provided by large whiskies to the despairing disillusion I shared with the latest pop groups' juke box dramas.

"Are you sure you'll be all right, Greg?" Thank God I was home! Eva stood silently, respectfully, as weak at the knees, I negotiated door and light.

Home. Two rooms with mod.cons., property of a member of Rowe's on a scholarship abroad, a dull place but briefly deified by memories of Laurel and our fleeting moments of love.

Eva watched shyly, spaniel-eyed. "Shall I come in and make some supper?" A pause and then, "I – er – could stay the night – ," (the girl was actually blushing), "Of course, I'll sleep on the settee."

"Of course!" I said and laughed.

"What's so funny, Greg?" she demanded indignantly.

I couldn't tell her that the vision of seducing her was quite riotously funny as well as unutterably obscene. Gently, momentarily conscience-stricken, I propelled her into the hall. "Goodnight, Eva. Thanks for everything. You've been very kind."

The door closed and I leaned against it weakly. Waiting.

Waiting for the moment that lay in ambush. Laurel was dead. She would not come again. Never to smile from the depths of the dim-lit room and eagerly stretch out her arms for me.

One dream could never come true. This room as I pictured it after she telephoned this morning, sending my hopes soaring, seeing our triumphant return, with a very different ending to this night.

The flat was safe now, safe from her clumsy, valiant attempts at housekeeping. Our love, now frozen by death into timelessness, would no longer be diminished by guilty feelings towards her sick mother. Within weeks, both mother and daughter were dead.

Both dead by violence.

As I poured out another whisky that set the pattern of many future meals, I thought about that violence. The police request for witnesses suggested that they weren't happy with the accident theory either. Where then did Laurel fit into the pattern? Negligence . . . or worse. Surely that was impossible. I refused to consider that my Laurel was capable of murder.

It was ironic. The heart operation had been a spectacular success, and Laurel's mother having been restricted for so long, had been able to live a full and active life. And then the accident happened, while she was accompanied by her only daughter.

The papers had loved the bit about all those tranquilisers she took. Had the habit of many years been too hard to break? Had she perhaps taken more than she should?

I jerked awake. Sleep was for the safe, the loved and the dead. Each time the whisky brought its merciful stupor of unknowingness, traffic noises momentarily quelled grew louder. I sat up sweating, as the blare of a horn and the scream of tyres brought the picture of Laurel falling. Falling . . .

CHAPTER THREE

It was morning. Outside it still rained and the room was as near daylight as the reluctant October gloom would make it. From the kitchen came the humane, familiar smell of coffee. Eva cheerfully clattered cups on to the table beside me, pretending not to notice my beat-up appearance and the rich aroma of many departed whiskies.

"How did you get in?" I said, sounding as inhospitable as I felt.

"You left the key in the door. I just turned it – and here I am." She sounded relieved, buoyant, the only person to be grateful that I was still alive this morning. Obediently I drank coffee, ate toast, agreed about the weather. A twelve-hour love-affair with the whisky had mercifully blunted the first abyss of despair, and raised the first subtle barrier between Gregor Roy MacGregor and the madness that lay with yesterday.

Fielding the empty whisky bottle into the waste paper basket, Eva boomed in her best hockey-playing manner: "Now, what shall we do today?" It was ten-thirty, and a little shiftily, she added, "Mr. Rowe isn't needing me today." She took a deep breath. "I might as well tell you, Greg, I came straight here from the enquiry." She put a restraining hand on my arm. "Actually I was nearer to her than you were. Just leaving the supermarket, I saw everything. They asked me and I said I'd go. You were so upset."

So yesterday was true. The words were spoken and I

could no longer will it away by pretending it didn't exist – hadn't happened.

Mistaking my shocked silence for disapproval, she said cautiously, "You don't mind, do you, Greg?"

(Mind! Oh, God!)

"Of course not. Thank you, Eva." My facial muscles were stiffening again with the effort of not crying. I thought of Laurel lying up there in the dreary shrouded house with its respectable lawns, the mouldy stone lions on the pathway making their feeble contribution to class and tradition.

"Shall we go out somewhere?" Eva asked.

"Have you some special treat in mind?" It was cruel and her plump face crumpled. "I'm sorry, Eva," I said, adding lamely, "Thought good secretaries had to hold the fort till the master cometh."

She murmured something about time for that when I recovered. So that's what they thought at Rowe's. That I needed to recover. Not from losing a beloved wife, of course, merely from the hallucination that she had ever been my wife, when she had so emphatically and persistently denied it.

Terrified at the prospect of another day with Eva and her boring, well-meant good-nature, I pleaded indisposition (which was pretty obvious) and politely eased her out of the flat. From the window I saw her tall muscular figure swing Amazon-like across the road and encased by the blue Mini car, drive away.

It had stopped raining. The small girl from downstairs danced along the street, shouting to the dashshund pup who scuttled anxiously, nose down, searching the antiseptic streets of Rowe's Vale hopefully for old insanitary lampposts.

A skittish pup. It struck a chord and sickened, I turned away, remembering the beginning. A hot afternoon in July . . .

CHAPTER FOUR

A hot afternoon in July.

Incredibly, time had existed before Laurel, a time when I was considered lucky, the winner of Rowe's nation-wide competition for an unknown artist to submit a mural for the new canteen in the new town of Rowe's Vale. "A substantial money prize is offered for an original idea to be executed in whatever medium the artist prefers . . . etc."

Fed up with teaching, grateful for even the effort of creating something for a change, I never thought of winning.

The complete disbelief that I had won lasted well into the gradual disillusion of the monstrous red-brick hell of Rowe's Vale, with the household word made manifest. The people themselves gave every indication of infesting the host as fleas owe loyalty to the individual dog they inhabit. With Rowe's houses, Rowe's shops, Rowe's to eat, drink and be merry with, a curious hypnotic existence ensued. And when they were in doubt, there were Rowe's mobile loudspeakers telling them how to vote, how to shovel snow, how to blow their noses.

The illusion of George Orwell's totalitarianism was quite wrong, too. This was a capitalist state at its uninhibited magnificent best. "A hundred years for Queen and Country and British to the very core." It was no idle boast, Rowe's meant every word of it.

The prospect of the mural brought its own gloom and despondency. There was scant inspiration in a landscape devoid of anything but serried ranks of red brick, a few choice well-planned ultra-modern hygienic parks and well-scrubbed playgrounds. And how did one compose ancestral portraits from small sepia postcards taken umpteen years ago? The men peering out from behind enormous moustaches and ferocious beards, like creatures in a thicket. The women, with tight-drawn lips and tight-drawn hair, and the kind of faces painted on wooden dolls, except that the dolls were invariably more attractive.

Even for Rowe's millions, a genuine portrait of the original ancestor who had arrived in the nearby Midland town penniless, from destination unknown, was a poser. This character, with more ingenuity than seat to his pants, tricked some misguided soul into lending him a decrepit garden shed and a few pounds. The first Rowe factory was born. The house and garden belonging with the shed, swiftly followed and their luckless, now penniless, original owner blew out his brains, all he had that was still his own property.

The only inspiration came from the beautiful doomed valley, shadowed as it was by the dam's great structure of white shining concrete, with neatly regulated towers like teeth in a giant's jawline. Behind those shining walls, in the subsidiary reservoir, the waters already gathered, waiting to be unleashed in the first part of the programme which by the following spring, would turn this valley into a water supply for Rowe's thirsty thousands.

To put it mildly, Rowe's would be extremely displeased at the valley taking prime place on their costly mural. Still, it was my clearest impression of Rowe's Vale. The summer sunlight on the tree-dappled twisting road, the hills and dales rising beyond it, and clustered like a palmful of sparkling gems, the stone-mullioned windows of exquisite ghosts of houses.

Before Laurel came, at weekends I thankfully watched the last of Rowe's Vale dwindling into the driving mirror of the hired car. The hot, obediently straight road softening, curving first to a milelong stone wall which disappeared between ornate lodge gates. After that, a dusty grey monotony of fields crouched behind blackened thorn hedges. The fields, fallow for seasons untold, and the bitter blighted look of neglect, characterised the country-side for a wide radius of Rowe's Vale.

Gaunt shells of cottages, coarse grasses bursting out between the broken spars of rotting fences, with gardens long past living memory of flowers, had an air of sinister abandonment. It was as if some great catastrophe had struck without warning. As if the inhabitants had fled into the redbrick oasis of the new town, lured by the false safety of coffee bars, supermarkets and the fleshpots of civilisation, all madly searching for fragments of that fairy gold associated with the magic word "Rowe's."

Then, quite suddenly, as though quit of a rather nasty enchanted forest, the scenery took a turn for the better and there were glimpses of a valley, and a slow river winding, sequined by sunlight. At the road-fork, a signpost lay, broken arms stretched skywards. The river fled behind the few stone houses clustered round an ancient village square.

An indecipherable inn sign, swinging in the slight breeze, was marvellously inviting. Past the broken sign-post, the car slid noisily and precariously down the track.

In the village, the inn sign was the only thing that stirred. The hospitality it offered was gone long since, door barred, windows taken over by a century of cobwebs and dead insects.

All around, neglected gardens, empty windows, told the same story as the houses on the upper road. And doubtless for the same reason – the lure of Rowe's ephemeral gold.

Ironically enough, the road still had some bite left in it. I cursed, drawing a fearsome long nail out of a rapidly diminishing tyre. Changing a tyre is hardly an uplifting spiritual experience at the best of times. Kneeling there, as birds sang and bright butterflies danced, whilst bees unseen went about their business, felt uncomfortably like being the only human left on earth.

In the absence of man, nature was coming into her own again. A broader, wider, less inhibited nature, about to give birth to some new species to take the place of wayward, self-destructive man. Man who would never listen to the warning signals from a dying planet.

The yellow afternoon light thickened and hardened into gold. A small ebony cloud, edged with scarlet lake, glided across the horizon.

The sense of peace, of timelessness, deepened, bringing a moment's wrath that humankind has such odd ideas of values.

"A tragic sight, is it not?"

I practically shed my skin and fled at that ghostly voice. An old man stood watching me, his leathery wizened face long past the appearance of mortal kind. Great hooded eyelids gave him an ancient saurian look and jutting craggy brows added to the unreality. Strands of white hair hung to his shoulders, and as the eyelids slowly moved, I saw his eyes were piercing palest blue, almost colourless.

"I thought the place was deserted."

The old man drew himself erect and there wasn't a single creak.

"The village will never be deserted as long as I live," he snapped as, eyes darting, he seemed to watch the way I was going to jump.

With that something only describable as "presence", he looked like the original King Lear, with a dash of Santa Claus without the genial "Ho, hos". The illusion wasn't helped by the ancient weapon he carried, the kind of blunderbuss I thought had disappeared with the Battle of Culloden.

15

Nervously, I wondered where he had dug that one up. More urgently, if it worked and noting the sullen angry expression with alarm, what the devil he intended doing with it.

CHAPTER FIVE

The old man's comforting antiquity was illusion too, for with a walk as light and springy as a youth's, he fairly bounded across the road, pointing out a house whose sundial and mullioned windows suggested William Shakespeare and Anne Hathaway.

"See the date – there, above the door? See it? 1588!"

I doubted that his eyes were that good. That periwinkle blue was partly the rheumy mists of age. "1588!" he repeated proudly. "That's when my family settled here. The year of the Armada."

He swung round to see how I was taking it. "Do you think I'm going to leave now, to go and live in that – hell!" And jerking an imperious hand towards Rowe's Vale, "So if they've sent you out here to tell me to pack up and leave, and enjoy their damned charity, you can go back and tell them I still intend to stay here whatever happens – d'ye hear – whatever happens?" And with that, he took a tighter grip on the gun as if to reinforce his argument.

"Steady on, now. I'm not from Rowe's. I'm not trying to persuade you to do anything."

"Then who are you?"

"Just a visitor. Saw the village and thought I could get tea at the inn."

"Oh! Is that so?" He didn't sound convinced. "All this land once belonged to the few families who settled this valley. Most of 'em farmers. Then that damned Rowe, he came and stole it, lied and cheated his way to every acre of it."

17

I was to learn that Rowe wasn't the last of his family to have a monopoly on lies and cheating, either.

"And not content with driving us out, d'ye know what his next move is?"

I knew all right, but at that moment ignorance seemed the better part of discretion. "He's going to dump us at the bottom of his damned reservoir. We're the prehistoric animals of Rowe's Vale, the dinosaurs. Some day someone will find these houses and our bones at the bottom of their lake. They'll send their archaeologists to dig us out, put us together again for their museums."

A jet flew overhead, drowning everything in its scream. Watching the white ribbon of its flight he added, "That's if they don't blow themselves to pieces first, Rowe and his like, the new rulers of the universe. Maybe it won't be humans after us, maybe some great intelligent insects for a change." His laughter wasn't any cheerier than his taste in guns.

I muttered about the National Trust protecting old houses.

"National Trust!" he echoed scornfully. "Against Rowe's?" He looked at me as if I'd suggested asking the Man in the Moon to lend a hand. "No one can go against Rowe's. What they can't buy, they steal or destroy to churn into their plastic horrors, their household gods."

Guiltily remembering how magnificent the dam had seemed, "a great feat of engineering, a modern marvel," they were calling it. "Oh indeed we're flooding some land. Nothing of value, of course."

Now the old man's sense of outrage communicated itself. For a moment I walked around inside his skin, old, thin and pitifully forgotten with a threadbare overcoat and boots so old and broken they let in the rain.

I shivered. The sun had put up his shutters, leaving the now enormous black cloud in sole possession of the sky. In the cool air, the old man's eyes watered

18

continuously. I saw an inevitable day when the pylons, marching relentlessly across mountain and glen, would come to rest at a peaceful croft by the side of a loch. And my home would be no more.

"How do you manage?" I asked. The three shops in my line of vision had not served a customer in this Elizabeth's reign. Some small concession to modernity had been chanced in the form of slot machines, now rusted and bearing brand names that had vanished before I left the nursery.

He smiled. "I can starve or go to their post office for my pension. Get my supplies then, don't need to go every week. You don't eat much at my age."

The prospect of Rowe's Vale was distant and far from pleasing. "But it's more than eight miles, there and back. What about bad weather? Winter?"

The ancient hooded lids jerked up, as if toying with the possibility that I was not after all an enemy. I fancied the grip on the blunderbuss slackened to "at ease." "There's a bus to the road end. What are you doing here anyway? You're a Scot!"

I held out my hand. "Gregor Roy MacGregor. I'm an artist."

"Thought so. I saw a photo of you in the paper the girl left."

Great heavy thunderdrops cut short any further conversation and a few moments later I was sheltering on the other side of the village sundial. At first I thought I was in a museum, then I realised this was where he lived.

The house had the musty smell of old men, stale tobacco and not a little dust and dry rot thrown in for good measure. Around me the natural beauty of mellowed oak beams was cluttered into oblivion. Ancient photographs and gloomy landscapes in heavy gilt frames fought for every inch of wall space. In dark corners wild animals, birds and fishes stared at us, trusting and forgiving from their glass tombs. Treasures in their time of many generations, they were supplemented by a rusted sword and cannon ball, a torn flag and drum, relics of the Battle of Vansett Bridge.

There was even a weighty locked family Bible, in which the family skeletons were immured before cupboards became fashionable. And regarding cupboards, even Mother Hubbard's dog was on his proverbial chinstrap here, for the old man was apologising at having "no refreshment to offer." This hadn't been the day for pension and supplies.

We talked of Scotland. I told him about the Glen, he told me about East Lothian where his grandmother had been born. The rain stopped.

"Perhaps you would come back another day?" he said wistfully. Then he was helping me change the tyre with astonishing dexterity, almost apologetically, one might say.

I took him into Rowe's Vale where he accepted supper at the Vansett Arms. Reluctant pride gave way to hearty appetite and a wealth of historical episodes concerning the area. Then, amid more protests, he was again deposited with shopping bag, heavy with a few pitiful necessities, beside the ruined signpost.

He wouldn't hear of me driving any further. "There might be more nails, you never can tell," he added with a sad saurian wink.

I looked at the valley, sunk in sleep. "What's going to happen to you when you have to leave?"

He rubbed his chin thoughtfully. "An old people's home, I suppose."

I knew it. I'd given a therapeutic demonstration on painting Christmas cards. A showbox with windows, full of antiseptic dormitories and the smell of hospitals. A few pathetic geriatrics with faces like ivory sunned themselves on its verandah on warm days. A daunting prospect for the senile and helpless, let alone a man with nearly a hundred years of memories and possessions to leave behind.

"Perhaps I can help you with your things, to move I mean, when the time comes."

"What time?" he demanded suspiciously. He sounded frightened.

"When they flood the valley. Where will you go?"

A wave of relief crossed his face, as he smiled away this ridiculous idea. "I shall stay here, of course."

I visited the Valley of the Dinosaurs often after that. One day the house looked and smelled surprisingly clean. It was tidy too with flowers neatly arranged in the windows. Unmistakeably the better for some female presence.

But Tom's sprightliness had gone. "It's my damned lumbago again. This terrible summer. That's what's caused it. Nothing but rain, rain, rain." And to my murmurs of sympathy, a brusque change of subject.

"Noticing my flowers, are you? You're my second visitor this week. Miss Smith was here yesterday." And back to the weather. "You should have seen the summers when I was your age. Marvellous they were. It's all this pollution, you know, that's what's changed the weather. I don't envy you young folk. No, not a bit."

Later that week, deciding he was too proud to ask for help, I collected some groceries and drove carefully down the steep road, wondering if Miss Smith was some part of an ancient romance.

Miss Smith! I foresaw an elderly dragon of dinosaur vintage.

A second later, I was furiously jumping on the brakes, the car screaming in protest. A small yellow pup stood in my path, staring indignantly, one paw delicately upraised, sniffing the air.

He had good nerves, that beast, better than mine, utterly indifferent to my curses.

21

I was revving up, swearing, when the dragon Miss Smith, was upon me.

A slicker getaway and I would never have met her, never married her. Never heard that other nightmare scream of brakes.

CHAPTER SIX

She stood smiling, a wraith in the twilight, with short silver-blonde hair, small and slender as a fairy-tale princess. Apologising, scolding and comforting the pup, who snuggled unharmed against her.

Instead of driving away with an indignant snort, I was rooted to the spot – bewitched, as she meant me to be – pretending suicidal dogs happened every day and that my nerves were made of steel. And all the time watching with distinct pleasure her ringless hands, caressing the pup's head.

Aye, the Enchanter himself was near at that moment, or maybe the fair witch whistled up the storm about our ears. For having said everything conventional and never having much gift of the gab in my slow Scots tongue, the blessed rain began to fall.

I invited her to sit in the car and wait. (God, did I really sound that curt and ungracious!)

Hesitating, looking first along the desolate valley, then to the main road far above us, trying to assess me, she remembered what she had been told about strange young men with cars. It was laughable until I knew there was more than naïvity about her indecision, hearing later about the kidnapping and the grim-faced silent man who promised candy at the end of the journey.

She seemed merely ingenuous, touchingly so. I put her out of her misery. "Tom Markham's a friend of mine. He had an attack of lumbago."

She interrupted with a silvery laugh – just a shade

relieved too. "Oh! You're a friend of Tom's. Save yourself the journey, he's out."

Holding the car door open, I said, "He's told me about you. You're Miss Smith." Making it sound persuasive, as if I knew all about her. "Get in! No point in getting drenched. I'll give you a lift home."

She darted one final anxious look along the valley, scrutinized me and decided that I had an honest face. The chances were she *might* not have to get out and walk.

She got in and I reversed the car back up to the main road. Sudden proximity turned us both speechless and we watched the road ahead as if our lives depended on it. She was wearing some woody kind of perfume which the rain had intensified. For all her smallness, she was what my brother would have unhesitatingly classed as "a lady". The much maligned words "sex appeal" might have been invented for her.

Rowe's Vale came into sight a few silent miles ahead. Before it swallowed us, the hedged road changed back again into the high stone wall with its ornate lodge gates.

"This is where I live," she said, indicating the cottage at the gate, and silently cursing precious time wasted on thought instead of deed, I stopped the car. The rain was still heavy. She didn't seem eager to move.

"You're a Scot, aren't you?" she said. "Here on a visit?"

"A working visit. Just for a few weeks."

She looked back along the road. The driving mirror reflected a dwarfed version of the dam. "That sounds fun. Are you an engineer?"

"No. A painter." (Did I have to sound so mono-syllabic?)

"What sort of a painter?" she asked patiently.

I told her about the mural and she turned with a look of new interest. "How fascinating!" Her eyes were surprisingly, vividly, blue, the lashes and brows darker and thicker than one would have expected with that pale cloud of hair. "Do Rowe's treat you well?" There was something else in her eyes now, the laughter of a secret joke.

"Fair!"

She nodded and seemed pleased. I switched off the wipers.

The car was very quiet. The rain had stopped. There was no excuse to linger, but she seemed as incapable of movement as I did. I was noticing other things, the cunning elegance of that casual sweater and skirt, the beautiful shoes – orangey-brown shades all skilfully blended. Even the pup, curled up asleep on her lap, blended with the ensemble!

"That's a bonny cottage," I said, not meaning it. "Who owns the estate?"

She gave a tinkling laugh. "Rowe's, of course! It was Sir Arthur's at one time." She looked full at me. "I must go." Her voice sounded soft and regretful. Suddenly my tongue untied and I was frantically making a date.

CHAPTER SEVEN.

"You might at least have kissed me goodbye, darling," Laurel grumbled next evening, by which time we had discovered (as I suspected from our proximity in the car), a rare and absolutely shattering physical attraction.

There was little entertainment to be found in Rowe's Vale. For quite different reasons, we both avoided the red-brick wilderness of the satellite town. Satellite to the enormous factory which sprang into seething, virile life, about thirty years ago, spreading its hungry tentacles for labour and land, from the adjoining town of Weschester.

We rarely went into town, spending our evenings in the flat or in Tom's valley and the dales beyond it, country that still belonged to the landed gentry. Even that wasn't safe from Rowe's, for as soon as the owners died off, in they stepped and grabbed what they could of the large family homes.

Laurel pointed out one of these houses, built by a steel magnate nearly a hundred years ago. The County Council had run it as a mental home – at a loss – until Rowe's acquired interests, building new wings and using part as a private hospital where members of the staff (and anyone else who could afford the nominal sum they asked) could obtain treatment or merely rest-up for a while.

The surroundings were idyllic, perched high on a hillside with a magnificent view across the dales. The approach lay over an old-world humpbacked stone bridge – Vansett Bridge – celebrating some general in the Cromwellian wars and his forgotten moment of glory.

Cradling Laurel so willingly in my arms, all the other girls I had ever known and loved, compared to this one like a penny candle to an atom bomb. What did I care that the stories she told about her background, the vague tales of her parents, weren't twice alike. There were no direct lies, everything she said *could* be fixed down to approximate truth – if you used a corkscrew as a measuring tape.

Even the secret circumstances of our marriage should have suggested something "gey queer" going on, but by that time, she had me where she wanted me, and Jezebel or Caesar's wife, my saner moments and the questions they demanded, had faded.

"Of course I love you, Greg darling. But what about Mother? I must see her over this heart operation. What else can I do? She hasn't anyone but me. Oh, let's get married before that, I don't want to wait until afterwards. Please, Greg . . ." And her eyes lit up, as if she had just thought it out, not planned it step by step all the way along, even to setting up the marriage proposal ready baited for me to swallow.

"You have to go back to Scotland, anyway," she said mournfully. I had indeed. The mural was still unfinished, it was a bigger job that we had thought, even uncomplicated by Laurel, and I was committed to a half-term's teaching back home, until they found a permanent replacement.

Laurel was stroking my hair and saying softly, "Just the minute Mother is well enough, I'll come to you."

I bit back the comment, "What if she's worse?" Laurel was all she had. An invalid for many years, after Laurel's father died (an "administrator" with Rowe's, said Laurel!), they had lived mostly in France. "Rowe's were very good to us," she said, not bothering to add that her mother *was* Rowe's, and so obsessed with that kidnapping attempt when Laurel was six, that she preferred living abroad incognito, where no one had heard of them.

All this secrecy became an additional hazard when the time factor was vital.

Our wedding was a sharp business-like deal with the registrar at Weschester, a special licence and two surprised passers-by acting as witnesses. A train to London.

A few days later, realising Laurel was really going home to Mother and I was returning to Scotland (and not liking either prospect), I said acidly, "How are you explaining this holiday, anyway?"

Taking off her wedding ring, she kissed it and put it carefully into her purse. "Oh, I was seeing Lorna. Surely I told you that!"

"Oh, yes. Lorna!" I said wearily.

Sometimes, quiet men who shone briefly in a war, regarded it as their moment of glory and became frightful bores with their reminiscences. Well, it was that way with Laurel. Lorna was her war, her solitary bid for freedom.

Lorna was the adored (and I suspected only) friend, met sick and penniless in Antibes after the premature ending of a particularly hectic "*affaire*" with the producer of a travelling theatre (where Lorna figured well down the list of "other parts were played by . . .").

She discovered that Laurel had a "voice" (privately, I considered her only discovery was the shrewd observation that she was on to a good thing). Laurel was bullied, persuaded, cajoled, into leaving home and Mother and in no time (and on Laurel's money), Lorna had them set up as a singing twosome in some very sleazy continental clubs.

It ended one night when the bus overturned on a steep Swiss road. Lorna, at the window, was badly cut about face and arms. Laurel, taken to hospital with shock and concussion, was returned in contrite tears to Mother, whose health thereupon deteriorated so rapidly that Laurel would never dare leave her again.

I began to hate Lorna some time before Laurel took one of our few precious afternoons to go halfway across

London to see her. With jealous indignation, I watched her carefully make-up her face and take even greater care than usual with her always immaculate "*toilette*." She was too excited and glowing to even notice my sullen disapproval.

"Come if you want to, darling," she said, kissing me a perfunctory goodbye, already half-way into her gloves. The too-late invitation was so obvious an attack of conscience that I was both angry and insulted. Murmuring something about girlish confidences, I said "no" rather sharply.

Her face brightened. "Sure, darling? Won't you change your mind? You'd love Lorna." She could afford to insist, knowing it was quite safe to do so.

I doubted very much that I would love Lorna, a type all too common in my far from sheltered life. I was no actor either, to gush enthusiastically as would be expected. Chances were I'd hate her and sit scowling, resisting Laurel's attempts to "jolly" me, by whispering "Please don't be wooden, darling . . ." We would have our first quarrel.

No! Rather play safe. Let Laurel keep her illusions about her marvellous friend. I would stay discreetly out of it.

I suggested a compromise. There was an art gallery I had read about, in the district which housed Lorna Blagdon, and they were keen on doing exhibitions of young unknowns. It would save two wasted afternoons, and sweeten my temper. Laurel seemed delighted and said yes. There would be plenty of time for me to meet Lorna later.

When I got back to the hotel at six, Laurel was sitting in a chair by the window with a worried, woebegone face.

"How was Lorna?" I asked cheerfully.

She shook her head. "Not there," she gulped, looking perilously close to tears.

29

"Wasn't she expecting you?"

"Er – no, not really." She looked evasive. "I hate writing letters, I always put it off. I meant to write, and then – well, I decided to surprise her."

"I expect you left a message, then. Oh, come on, darling, it's not the end of the world," I said impatiently. "She'll get in touch with you."

Laurel stared sadly out of the window. "I didn't leave a message. The landlady thinks she's away on holiday. I won't see her, that's all." Then she abruptly changed the subject with the mercurial swiftness that always dazzled me. The whole gamut of emotions from tragedy to comedy, as effortlessly as Rachmaninoff rattling off a few scales.

Afterwards, I often wondered suspiciously if she had really spent that afternoon with Vic. Whether Lorna really existed. Except that I knew the colour of her hair and eyes, her amoral tendencies and the scrapes they got her into. Her odd talents, wonderful figure even her sole defect. "Poor Lorna's colour blind. It's quite rare in a woman, isn't it?" boasted Laurel. "She's a disaster when it comes to matching subtle shades, poor lamb." And prattling happily, she mistook my jealous gloom for interest.

So Laurel went home and I boarded the Intercity at King's Cross, feeling distinctly foolish carrying an enormous brown-paper parcel, having given Laurel my only suitcase.

To keep Mother unsuspecting, she had travelled to London lightly, too lightly alas for a bride, and we had hardly got into Regent Street before she was regretting "nothing pretty to wear." The ensuing shopping spree rapidly produced an expensive trousseau, hardly compatible with the inside of one quite small weekend case. Somehow, we never thought about mundane things like packing. When we did, it was Sunday night.

30

"Oh, have my case," I said, "You can't travel to Rowe's Vale behind a mountain of dress boxes."

So she took it, the suitcase which was to play its own macabre part later on.

CHAPTER EIGHT

Back home in Scotland, I could hardly contain myself. I was thinking of the bombshell when Laurel arrived that October, hearing myself saying, "I want you to meet my wife."

How it would shatter Callum, this hearty practical-joking, elder brother of mine, with his earthy comments on not having a girl, for being too shy and unforthcoming with women.

I could hardly wait.

It was as well to have some consolation, some justification for those lonely weeks, the almost daily quarrels with Callum. Even painting the mural was rosy in retrospect, infinitely preferable to the soullessness of teaching art to children whose ardent desires and inclinations lay in more mundane, active fields.

My main worry, however, was lack of communication with Laurel. Nearly three months was a long time to be parted, without even letters to look forward to. First of all, she said she hated writing, besides her mother might find out. Oh, they might be travelling around, probably back to Antibes for a few weeks to let Mother recuperate.

Finally, when I insisted on writing, she grudgingly suggested a *"post restante"* at Rowe's Vale. Then with a gentle laugh, she soothed away my anger. Of course she loved me, but surely I could see it *might* be awkward, particularly as Mother often opened her mail since the Lorna episode. When I protested indignantly, Laurel merely smiled, and gave that small Gallic shrug. "What is there for her to see, anyway, I have no secrets?"

As a compromise she would send post-cards whenever, where ever she could manage, adding tenderly, "Don't look so cross and sad, darling. It isn't for ever. After October, we'll be together always. No more secrets to hide – nothing."

Needless to say, no post-card ever arrived.

The arrangement was that Laurel would arrive in Edinburgh off the night train from London on the morning of October 22nd. My duties at the school finished on the 21st and I would be there to meet her, to start a new life. At this time I still naïvely believed in immediate success, on the strength of the award from Rowe's!

Even Edinburgh Waverley Station, at that hour in the morning an empty echoing tomb, could not quell my excitement. The drizzle of autumn dawn, with the Castle sullenly withdrawn above misty rocks, gleaming like patent leather, fairly seethed with the romance of departed ages.

The train was on time. It glided smoothly along the vibrating platform. Doors slid open and passengers emerged, heads well down in the early morning chill. The crowd thinned, a few stragglers remained.

Then with something like panic, I realised that was the lot.

Laurel! Laurel? Unbelievingly, I ran down the platform.

The train curved down the track like a sleeping monster, exhausted and happily at rest beside the empty platform. Cleaners bustled past, and I got some coy looks for craning my neck over the railings for a closer look at the train.

Of Laurel, there was not a sign.

"She isn't there! She isn't there!" My mind registered the words over and over with angry disbelief.

I never realised, until Enquiries told me that that *was*

the night train, that hearts literally do sink. Mine had gone so far as to be somewhere in the region of my feet. With legs weak and heavy all at the same time, Waverley Steps so eagerly descended, became an Everest to surmount. The morning's romance had died behind a surly face and changed into a vale of tears.

The hotel bedroom brooded high over the noisy, hissing, steaming, vibrating station. I sat by the window, chain-smoking nervously to the detriment of an already aching throat and telephoning the station at regular intervals. There was no message.

Between trains I made and rejected a dozen fantastic theories about *why* she hadn't arrived, avoiding of course, the one which was strikingly obvious!

Telephone contact with the now hardly civil Enquiries was no longer sufficient. After personal inspection of every train from London, even my optimism was thin. But fool's paradise still intact – ("Anyone can miss a train, perhaps I got the days confused – how we'll laugh about it later," I told myself), knowing she would come next day, or at worst, if something had happened to Mother, surely there would be a message care of the station master by tomorrow.

The aching throat had now progressed into the next stage, a streaming nose, plus a vague feeling that the top of my head might go into immediate orbit on its own account.

But nothing was coming between me and that train at six a.m.

How similar are the night travellers, I concluded, as bleary-eyed from a sleepless, feverish night, I watched once more the crowd disperse.

A head, bobbing distantly, looked like Laurel, but wasn't. At that setback, my temperature began boiling the mercury. The cleaners gave me knowing looks. As the last solitary porter whistled his way down the empty platform, I tottered to the bookstand, in search of a bottle of aspirins.

I saw a newspaper headline: "Train Sensation."

Deeply involved with trains, living and breathing them for the last two days, bound in sympathy to anyone who also suffered by them, I read on:

"Tragic accident on train. Enquiry on Rowe heiress . . ."

CHAPTER NINE

It was the unimaginable answer to all those theories. Rowe's and the train were too much of a coincidence.

"Yesterday afternoon at the enquiry into the death of Lady Marsden-Smith, widow of Sir Arthur Marsden-Smith of Rowe's Ltd, a verdict of accidental death was recorded.

Lady Marsden-Smith recently underwent an exceedingly rare heart operation from which she made a brilliant recovery. At the time of the accident she was returning from London after a final checkup, accompanied by her only daughter Laurel, who stated that her mother left the carriage 'to go to the loo.' When she did not return, Miss Marsden-Smith went into the corridor where she noticed one of the train doors was open. Unable to find her mother she gave the alarm.

Lady Marsden-Smith's body was found ten miles back near the railway line. As there were no witnesses to the accident, it was presumed that, feeling faint, she attempted to open a window and opening a door by mistake was drawn out by the air-stream.

Laurel Marsden-Smith stands to inherit the Rowe fortune on her twenty-fifth birthday. Her mother, a celebrated beauty of the 'fifties, was the only daughter of Cecil Rowe, grandson of the founder of Rowe's . . ."

Skipping a paragraph about the firm:

"Dr. Gerald L. Fellton, physician to the family, stated that he was prevented from returning by the same train, because of an emergency meeting at the hospital. He told

the enquiry that Lady Marsden-Smith normally travelled long distances by train as she suffered from carsickness.

Asked whether the recent operation would have contributed to her feeling of debility, Dr. Fellton re-emphasised that her health had been perfect since the operation. To the question of her being under drugs, Dr. Fellton stated that she had taken sleeping pills for many years and normally had in her possession tranquillisers of a harmless nature similar to those on the market for travelsickness.

In conclusion, Dr. Fellton assured the court that the cause of death was a fractured skull, not an overdose of drugs . . ."

There was a lot more, but the words were behaving in an odd way.

"Are you all right, sir? Can I get you a taxi?" a porter asked anxiously. Clutching the newspaper, mouth suddenly stiff and sore, I murmured the address.

At the hotel, someone, presumably a doctor, neatly precipitated me into hospital, where I presently lay absorbing anti-biotics and the dubious satisfaction that Laurel Smith (or Marsden-Smith) had loved me for my self alone.

It was something akin to the shock of winning the Mint in a raffle (and practically the same financially) to realise that, in blissful ignorance, I had married Rowe's!

Several lights now glimmered in the darkness, one that gave me immense pride was that Laurel perhaps thought me too proud to marry an heiress.

When I was as nearly normal as hospital could make me, Big Brother Callum came, grumbling as usual, to gather up the debris. All the way home, his handsome over-florid face bursting angrily, he blamed it on "a' that daft painting", as if I had wilfully encouraged pneumonia by painting the Forth Bridge without my overcoat.

Seeing myself reading all the waiting letters from Laurel, I relaxed and pretended deafness. Aye, it would be good to be home, with the morning glitter of sun on Loch Ogie, and the wind blowing the heather.

There was no letter from Laurel. Nothing.

There was a post-card from Eva in Madrid, and an invitation to do an exhibition at the Treasure Trove Art Gallery.

As a signal of success, its timing could not have been arranged with greater irony.

Things got worse. That evening I had a fight with Callum, when I insisted on walking down to the village. I had to telephone Laurel. Obviously she needed my support in her anguish.

When Callum snapped "What lass is this?"

I said, "Laurel. The girl I'm married to."

He stared. "Married? You!" Then he roared. "Dinna kid me, Gregor Roy. Ye're no married to anybody." Then suddenly anxious. "Ye're feeling well enough, are ye, now? Ye're no' going t' hae a relapse?"

Furiously, I marched out of the house. Why the devil hadn't she written? As a suitable scapegoat for her apparent oversight, the village postie, trudging home, nicely fitted the bill.

"Nay, nay, there was naething, naething at a', Meester Gregor," He eyed me curiously, "An' are ye a wee thing better the now?" As if asking for post were a symptom of my damned illness!

In the only telephone booth in Glen Ogie, which offered the benefits of icy winds blowing through its broken windows and a fine view of rain-sodden, burnt umber hillside, I made the first of many calls to Laurel Marsden-Smith.

With an ostrich-like determination that all would be well, I put down the hostile reluctance in the female voice at the other end to the possibility that here was yet another reporter.

"Miss Marsden-Smith is not available."

38

"You mean she's not in?" I said, sounding angry and impatient.

The voice turned cold. "She isn't available. You can call later, if you like." As she sounded like hanging up, I said,

"Did you tell her it was Greg?"

"I'm sorry. Miss Marsden-Smith is not at home. I'll give her your message."

Back at the croft, I cursed the parsimonious streak in Callum that "wouldna' waste his guid money on they 'phones and sich-like." Here we were in the twentieth century, surrounded by the wonders of atomic power and space travel, enjoying the same isolated splendours that Bonnie Prince Charlie doubtless encountered, right down to the identical plumbing.

My relations with Callum did not improve by his unfortunate tendency of staring at me, muttering "Married, b'God!" and choking with ill-advised humour.

Later that week I went into the byre to hear one of his cronies remarking, "D' ye no' think the laddie's a wee thing simple?"

That decided me. Next morning, with Callum in the top field helping the vet deliver his prize cow, I slipped out and a wearying day and night later, trudged into Rowe's Vale.

By a stroke of fortune, the flat was still mine. A cheery letter awaited that the owner was extending his stay in the States.

Now for the unavailable Miss Marsden-Smith.

Beyond the lodge gates (where the orange pup, now almost grown, barked at the window), the gloomy Edwardian house was characteristic of the marriage between sudden wealth and lack of taste. As a final insult to turrets, gargoyles and other tortuous medieval embellishments, the door was guarded by two hideous leprous stone beasts, holding the remains of heraldic documents in their forepaws. They yawned openly (perhaps in need of a good library subscription), and, showing a dentist's nightmare of decayed stone teeth, turned their blind, choleric gaze on poor demented travellers who must pass between them.

The entrance itself suggested a vulgar décor for Beauty and the Beast. As the bell rang hollowly, Frosty Voice opened the door. Behind her crouched partially shrouded furniture, giving an uncomfortable impression of a hall caught out in its shuddering underwear.

It doesn't seem possible, but I got even less change face-to-face than on the telephone. Frosty Voice had an eye to match. Too elegant for maid or housekeeper, she was undoubtedly a relative.

Our mutual appraisal suggested mortal combat. It started with exquisite politeness: "Will you please tell Laurel that Greg is here?"

"Laurel?" The well-drawn eyebrows quivered. "Laurel?"

"Yes! Tell her that her husband, Gregor, is here."

The elegant mask cracked slightly.

"Husband?" she gasped.

"Yes. Husband. Didn't she tell you she was married?"

"Married?" The carmine-painted mouth dropped open.

It was all very tedious, like watching Chekov done by the fourth form in the village school. I lost my temper.

"Yes, madam, married. If we're finished with the question and echo game, perhaps I can come in and talk to my wife."

The spell was broken and looking as if she had come face-to-face with an escaped lunatic, or a door-to-door salesman of the persistent variety, the door slammed smartly.

Too late with my foot, I viciously assaulted the bell, hearing with utmost satisfaction its angry screeching through shrouded furniture and empty space.

At last Frosty Voice returned. Under the enamel, her face was quite pink. "I don't know what your game is," she said, "but if you don't go away immediately, I shall call the police."

"Wait a moment, Aunt Judith!"

She turned swiftly, and peering past her shoulder, I caught a glimpse of pale silvery hair.

Laurel. Wearing the housecoat I bought her in London.

My heart's agonised lurch of joyful recognition and relief swiftly faded. Cold, gnawing anguish took its place. She looked ill, pale and queer. Like someone newly out of a sickbed.

"Please go away and don't make a fuss," she pleaded, watching me from the shadows, and her voice was the only firm thing about her. "We don't mean to – to hurt you, but really, I'm certainly *not* married to you." She craned her neck forward, for a better look, then laughed. The silvery laugh I remembered so well. "What a fantastic idea!" she said, "Who are you? I've never seen you before. You're not from these parts, are you?" And quite unabashed, she darted her aunt a look of triumphant innocence.

"Never mind who he is, Laurel," cut in Aunt Judith sharply, "Go right inside. You shouldn't be standing about in the cold." And as I stood there staring breathlessly at Laurel – my beautiful adored Laurel – beautiful female Judas, the door was one more, quite finally, slammed in my face.

CHAPTER TEN

In the flat, I let out the stale air with the staler dreams. Then, finishing a bottle of whisky (opened in the rapturous long-ago with Laurel), I clearly and candidly examined the situation.

There was absolutely no doubt, and I could certainly prove (I thought), that Laurel was my legal wife. In fact, had Laurel been plain Laurel Smith I might have rushed back at that moment and forcibly abducted her. But what had I to offer the heiress of Rowe's millions?

There must be some reason for her fantastic denial. Perhaps second thoughts? Did she think, or worse, had she been *persuaded*, that knowing from the outset who she was and, a base adventurer, I was merely after her money?

Going deeper into the pit, left two alarming alternatives. She was a schizophrenic or, remembering her subtle crafty vagueness, I had provided a rich girl's escapade, a vicarious trip into the world normally only seen fleetingly from the back of a Rolls.

The quiet wedding with unknown witnesses, her insistence on the utmost secrecy, all fitted that diabolical theme. Her concern for her mother, what the shock might do, was macabre enough now. Better the swift heart attack than the messy business of falling off a train at seventy miles per hour, I thought callously.

And how well I had played along. Enslaved, marvelling that she actually wanted to marry me, I had thrust natural caution and unspoken questions aside as irrelevant. Even my natural secretiveness had worked against me. Inwardly groaning, remembering brother Callum's reactions to the news that his "wee brother" had married an heiress, I shuddered at the damning testimony of the Glen Ogie folk who had known me all my life. They would shake their heads: "A strange-like laddie. Out painting at a' hours and in a' weathers. Aye, a wee thing simple, ye ken." And if they were more charitable, the victims of more recent encounters, like the postie and the lass on the telephone exchange, could hardly feel so well-disposed.

What would be Eva's reaction, for instance? Eva with her respect and awe for the Rowe's household gods. Her complete subservience and respectful salaaming of her boss, who was only remotely connected with the original Rowe clan. Eva's reaction could be summed up in one word. Disbelief. "Gregor's a crackpot sometimes," she would chuckle indulgently, with a fond shake of her head.

There was Tom Markham. Laurel and I had seen him often before our marriage. Well, I had no heart to bring him into this, to share my disillusion. A poor lonely old man grateful for a benevolent and charming Miss Smith. What if he found that she was in fact Rowe's, the despised, the loathed? The charitable offerings mere assuagement of guilt at destroying him. No, Tom had so little left, let him at least keep some illusions.

But supposing – supposing *all* these theories were wrong. That there was another answer. I remembered the feeling of oneness we both experienced right from the beginning. As Laurel expressed it, "two halves of one being. It was like being half-finished before you came." Banal, perhaps. Expressed by many better lovers in many better words. But nevertheless true.

Why then had she ceased to love me? And seeing again her pale, vacant face watching wraithlike, out of the gloom, I had an inspiration.

43

What if she hadn't *consciously* ceased to love me at all? What if, blaming herself as the indirect cause of her mother's death, hysterically blaming our relationship as the cause of a superstitious judgment on her, she had suffered a breakdown – a loss of memory?

Why had I not thought of it before? This was the perfect answer to her odd behaviour. Naturally, no relative, no loyal Rowe-ite, concerned with money and the possible hereditary neurosis of their offspring, was going to pass on that information. You don't accrue millions without discretion of a magnitude to make child's play of deception.

There must be someone who could sympathise – who could discreetly confirm my suspicions. Some trusted servant. What about her doctor? He would surely welcome any possible means of restoring her memory.

Shoved in my painting knapsack was the crumpled newspaper with the account of the accident. Opening it again, the deadly chill of that morning in Edinburgh Station swept over me. The chill of foreboding.

"Fellton. Dr. Gerald L. Fellton."

CHAPTER ELEVEN

Dr. Fellton's surgery lay in the gigantic block of offices and supermarkets which served Rowe's Vale as a town centre. There was also a large geometrically disciplined car park, whilst a few well-balanced trees, protected by wire shrouds from the unwelcome attentions of dogs, constituted a park.

Frail seemed the chances of any good-going germ surviving the length of those hygienic and antiseptic stairs, let alone the waiting-room which offered enough astringent comforts of chrome and formica to keep any microbe's mind off procreation. Presumably Rowe's Valians were healthy, for I had the consulting hour to myself and it was almost over when I saw Dr. Fellton get out of his car, carrying golf clubs.

He seemed very surprised to find a patient waiting and at my name he didn't bat an eyelid. Considering my recent illness, tales of debility were not altogether untruthful.

Taking pulse and temperature, his physical nearness confirmed the advertised qualities of mouthwash, deodorant, after-shave lotion, hair-cream – the lot. The sanitized odour of an affluent society.

Pulse and temperature declared normal, with professional appraisal and the desk between us, he asked some leading questions about my work (did I like being at Rowe's, were they good to me, etc.?) His laconic reception of my replies warned that he was used to sorting out malingerers.

Fellton was both younger and smarter than I had

imagined the Rowe family doctor to be. A big man, with a complexion that would be florid some day, when success (or excess) turned a well-muscled body to fat. The smooth dark hair grew rich and low on his forehead. He would have been remarkably handsome but for the dead fish stare of his pale blue eyes. They struck a chord somewhere.

As he wrote a prescription, I murmured something about the train tragedy and said, "Has Miss Marsden-Smith recovered now?"

His brisk and professional "Taking it very well, you know," gave nothing away.

Made bolder by desperation, I said: "Her loss of memory is purely temporary, I suppose."

He put down his pen. He looked astonished, but certainly not struck by the thunderbolt I had intended.

"Loss of memory! My dear fellow, whatever makes you say that?" He laughed, slapping his thigh, obviously enjoying the daftness of the idea. "As far as I know Miss Marsden-Smith, except for a slight chill, is in perfect health. There is certainly nothing wrong with her memory." Archly, conspiratorially, he added, "Now where did you hear that?"

I supposed around the works somewhere.

He tch-tched sadly. "Isn't it amazing the stories people will invent for sheer effect? How on earth could they have got hold of an idea like that? It seems that no one's ever happy with the ordinary. As if the accident wasn't enough of the sensational to whet anyone's appetite." He sighed and stood up, handing me the prescription. "This should put you right. If you have any more trouble, come back and see me." His "Good afternoon," firm and friendly, was nevertheless dismissal.

I gave him one more chance. "You may be interested to hear that I know Laurel Marsden-Smith extremely well."

He smiled affably, spreading his hands in an expansive

gesture. "She has many friends." That was a lie, for a start.

"This was different. We were hardly friends. We happen to be married."

He didn't even flinch. "Really?" he said cautiously.

"Yes, really. Think it over. You know where to find me if you need me again."

He looked very thoughtful as I closed the door.

CHAPTER TWELVE

Even seen with the unprejudiced eye of reassessment, the mural in Rowe's canteen was nothing more than a blatant, rubicund, piece of propaganda, boosting the rags-to-riches theme so near to Rowe's heart. Muscular heroic figures, the smoking factory chimneys, the small shed of its sacred nativity, crowded the canvas. The sentiments portrayed were "You can do this, if you're British, truthful, honest, clean," in that order!

Family portraits, eked out of ancient sepia photos (where they existed at all), were humanised out of all recognition. Tenderising cold-eyed, tight-lipped Sir Arthur's expression, I wondered where Laurel had got her fragile beauty from. Presumably Laurel's mother had not always looked like a well-bred horse.

Painting and whisky provided a fifty-fifty occupational therapy, keeping me from going clean daft over Laurel's betrayal. I almost fell off the ladder when Eva twittered "Well, you are a stranger, you are." And the treacle-brown eyes, bovine at eye level, were charmingly winsome and girlish seen through a whisky haze, from far above. Muscles, height, were diminished into an illusion of fragility.

My penchant was obviously for small delicate females and basely, I would doubtless have adored Eva if she had been nearer five feet than six and hadn't wanted to boss me around all the time.

As if thought-reading, she said reproachfully. "You

should have let me know you were coming back. I would have got the flat ready."

I mumbled something about it being unexpected, that I had been ill – a dose of 'flu.

Standing back a little better to study my ravaged countenance, she shrieked "Oh, I do hope you haven't come back too soon. You're not looking a bit well."

Huffily reassuring her, I turned my back rudely and dabbed away at Sir Arthur, in absorbed and dedicated silence.

Eva dithered, chatting about holidays (had I got her card from Madrid?) and finally drifted off, dragging her large feet like a sad, sick elephant. I flung down the brush, conscience-stricken. There was no need to take it out on Eva, who for some curious reason, always wanted to be friendly.

Down the corridor, in a glass-fronted office marked "Hartley Rowe, Managing Director", Eva gloomily contemplated her typewriter, so downcast that I felt six feet of heel all the way. Poor Eva, potentially a good wife for somebody (how brother Callum would smack his lips over that "fine figure of a lassie!) Perhaps if I told her the truth about Laurel, she would stop wasting her time on me.

After a film that evening, we went back to her flat. I had to hand it to Eva. Most women in love would have had hysterics, sworn or thrown something. But for a good old British stiff upper lip, Eva was hard to beat. Rowe's would have been proud of her, it was in their best tradition!

Without even a semi-quaver in her voice, she marched into the kitchen and brewed another pot of coffee. I followed her and said lamely, "Well, what do you think?"

She smiled brightly. "So she denies it completely, does she?"

I said the marriage could be proved, and Eva exploded. "Why? Why bother?"

"Because she's my wife. Because I love her, Eva."

49

At such sentiment, Eva curled a black-downed upper lip scornfully. Measuring out the coffee with elaborate care, she said, "Tell me, how long were you ill in Scotland, Greg? It wasn't *really* 'flu, was it?"

When I told her, she nodded eagerly. "Uh-huh!"

"What do you mean, uh-huh?" I demanded angrily. Then the horrible truth descended. "Eva, for God's sake! Surely you don't think I'm making it all up?"

Avoiding my eyes, she seemed to be thinking hard for an answer. "Actually," she said slowly, choosing her words, "I think you're either a villain – or a sick man." Letting that sink in, she added, "I'd prefer to believe you're sick."

"I don't see what you're getting at."

"I think you do, Greg. Yes! I think you do. It's blackmail, isn't it? It's hard for me to associate you with such a vile thing, but there it is. You'll never get away with it, a fantastic stunt like pretending you're secretly married to Laurel Marsden-Smith – with Rowe's!" It was exactly as if she had said "With God!"

I groaned. What sacrilege had been committed in her eyes. No wonder she preferred me sick. "All right, Eva. If you'll drive me into Weschester tomorrow morning, I'll prove I'm speaking the truth."

That drive was anything but companionable. Eva drove sullenly, ominously silent. Occasionally glancing at her, I saw her chewing all her lipstick off. A sure sign of nerves with Eva.

However, I found the sight of Weschester's sprawling streets most refreshing, stirred by its rich untidy history, which had taken seven hundred years to produce the present squalor and overcrowdedness. How endearing its sheer unsanitary corners, after the antiseptic modernity of Rowe's Vale.

At the Registrar's Office, Eva looked more apprehensive than ever, especially when the clerk spread the entry before us. Obviously curious, he regarded Eva doubtfully, then a tiny smile twitched across his face. He tipped me the ghost of a secret wink. ("We were men of the world, we were".)

"Laurel Smith, 21. Rowe Lodge." (Parents: A. Smith, decd. Celia Smith – housewife). Underneath: "Gregor Roy MacGregor, 28. Artist. Parents deceased."

Eva couldn't get out quick enough. In the car, I was amazed at the angry tears in her eyes. "Oh, Greg, how could you? What on earth do you hope to gain by such a deception? If it's money, you could have borrowed from me. You *are* in some terrible trouble, aren't you?" She grasped my arm. "Oh, you poor thing!"

"Eva, listen to me. The only trouble I'm in is speaking the truth that no one will believe. It must be obvious, even to you, that I did marry someone. Who is she then? And where is she, for that matter? How do you explain my missing bride, if it wasn't Laurel Smith?"

She shuddered. "I don't know! I don't know!" And sniffing pathetically all the way back to Rowe's Vale, she announced in a voice of doom, "I've shopping to do. See you later." Driving into the car park, she dislodged her shopping bag from its needful sole occupancy of the back seat. As I got out, there, sitting alongside us at the wheel of a neat and costly red sports car was Laurel Marsden-Smith.

I would hardly have known her, for she was wearing dark glasses and her fair hair was hidden under a frantically-hued headscarf. What I did recognise was the expensive and elegant coat I bought her on our honeymoon.

I gripped Eva's arm. "Here's someone I want you to meet."

Dragging back, obviously unwilling, her awed whisper sibilant: "Greg, that's Laurel Marsden-Smith! Greg, please. Don't make a scene." Eva tried hard to appear small, indistinguishable, not with me, whilst I held on to her and said, "Hello, Laurel! Perhaps you recognise me today."

The face turned its blank anonymous stare, but somewhere around the mouth there was a short quiver of fear. "No!" She shook her head violently. "No!" then dully, "Oh, yes, you're the fellow who thinks I'm married to you."

"Yes, Laurel. And it happens to be true."

Behind the dark glasses, the blue eyes widened. "You're crazy! I'd never seen you until you came to the house with that ridiculous story. I should surely know if I'm married or not. Look here, you'd better stop pestering me, or I'll call the police."

Eva tugged violently at my sleeve. Briefly her face peered round, all apology to the girl in the car. "Please don't do that. He doesn't know what he's saying. He's been ill, you know . . ."

I could have smacked her, making me feel idiotic – the tenant with the mortgage foreclosed.

Laurel shrugged. "I'm sorry, but it's a bit thick, isn't it? It's – it's awful!"

"Hello! What's awful, my dear?" And there was the boss himself standing behind us. Mr. Hartley Rowe. "Ah, good morning, Miss Black." He tipped his hat to Eva, who was practically curtseying in return. Then, smile broadening, he held out his hand. "Well, MacGregor, didn't recognise you for a moment! You know Laurel?" His eyes were tragic triangles under weighty black brows in a chalk white face. A clown's face. Small, rotund, a poor figure of a man, a face like that on anyone else would have been ridiculous, but he managed to make his whole presence sleek and smooth and shining. And by money's presence, infinitely respectful.

52

Blissfully unaware of the atmosphere, he was introducing us, but Laurel already had the engine running. "Please, Uncle Hartley. Let's go."

Rowe's eyebrows twitched. He seemed surprised at the way the party was shaping. "Oh, very well. Cheerio, MacGregor. Mural progressing all right? Good, good! Must come and have a drink with us sometime." He had hardly got the door closed when the car leaped away. Driving like a demon was a new aspect of Laurel's character, remembering her careful respect for the hired car.

Eva wrenched free from my hold, stammering with rage and embarrassment. "Oh – oh – oh, how could – you be – so – so – beastly?" She stamped her foot, and with a look of pure hate, dashed off into the doors of Rowe's most super supermarket.

CHAPTER THIRTEEN

Grimly I worked on the mural. The echoing silence of a Saturday afternoon in an empty building was broken by the distant tat-tap of a typewriter. Behind her glass partition sat Eva.

Rather coldly, she said it was the end of the financial year, everybody was working overtime but Mr. Rowe had asked her to come in at weekends also, and simpering with ill-concealed pride "As a special favour to him."

Interrupted by an angry buzz, she snatched a paper out of the machine and rushed towards Rowe's door. Turning, she said, "Sorry about this morning, Greg. I'll – I'll try to understand, if you give me time." Another buzz. Rowe seemed to expect jet-propelled office workers too.

That evening I went to visit Tom Markham. The valley had changed from the gentle greens and blues of summer to the harsh aching loveliness of autumn. All around trees died in the stark poignant beauty of cadmium yellows and chrome orange, and what had been luscious and fertile now lay sourly brown and fallow, with the decay of the year's ritual death.

There was an added sadness knowing that the small animals were busily prepared for their winter sleep, in ignorance that for them there would be no spring-time awakening.

Even Tom looked different – sadder, and if it were possible, even older. He at least seemed glad to see me, and eventually asked:

"Do you still see Miss Smith, by the way? I was

wondering what had become of her. Hasn't been down here since you went away."

My doleful shake of the head was significant enough for the slow eyelids moved, "I thought she was a fine girl for you," and he quickly changed the subject to his pet theme. Rowe's insistence that he go immediately to the old folk's home so that they could demolish some of the larger houses in the valley. And of course, his refusal to do so.

In less than two weeks the valley would be flooded, and all I had achieved for Tom, was his promise to stay in the flat until he found somewhere else – "when the time came." (How carefully we avoided direct reference to the end. Like knowing someone had an incurable disease.) Tom accepted my plan with almost suspicious docility, I thought.

Walking back down the road to Rowe's Vale, past Laurel's home, the lodge seemed deserted and the gates, when I tried them, locked. I was disappointed, dimly recognising that the idea of confronting Laurel again had been behind the idea of this long walk home.

Suddenly my own future seemed as bleak as Tom's. Certain that commissions would immediately follow the award at Rowe's, I had been only too eager to resign my teaching job. Well, the solitary offer of an exhibition indicated pretty pointedly that my aspirations to success were somewhat premature. One thing was abundantly clear – whatever happened, the past life with Callum at home in Glen Ogie was forever closed to me.

Considering all things, it was just as well that I hadn't the upkeep of an expensive wife, remembering how my eyes had widened at Laurel's extravagant tastes in London. She had bought one coat costing more, I fancied, than Callum's lifetime expenditure on clothes. And not finished there, calmly considered four equally expensive *ensembles* all on the same day. In retrospect, this indifference to money was all that might have indicated Laurel's wealthy background. For the rest, she behaved like any girl who had hitherto led a somewhat sheltered life, and like any girl in love, saying the same extravagant things open to rich or poor.

What in heaven's name had made her marry me? And the trapped animal was frantically running wild in its tiny cage again. If only I could get her to talk to me.

If only. If only . . .

Then, like the answer to a prayer for a miracle, when I opened the door of the flat, a faint beam from the reading-lamp on the desk touched someone who crouched, waiting in the shadows . . .

"Laurel!"

CHAPTER FOURTEEN

"Laurel!"

Even as I said the words, I wondered how on earth she had got in. Then I remembered. The key!

Of course! I had given her the other key long ago.

My face began tingling with excitement. This was absolute conclusive proof that she had told a pack of lies about not being married to me.

Her presence could mean only one thing. Marvelling at my turn of fortune, I reached out for the main light switch.

She cried out. "Don't, Please," and blowing her nose, added in muffled tones. "Please, Greg. My face is a mess. I've been crying."

"Darling!"

With a small shuddering movement, she withdrew back into the shadows. "Please, Greg. Listen. Will you?"

I made to sit by her, but she gave a husky laugh. "No! Over there. I'm not sure that I can talk sensibly with you so near." And the sudden determined twist away from me was like a slap in the face.

No longer so sure of my good fortune, I sat down wearily.

"Well, what's it all about? Why all the lies?"

"Wh – what lies?" She looked surprised. My God – surprised!

"Come on you know what I'm talking about. You know perfectly well that we're married. How did you get in here, if you haven't got a key? Or do you think I distribute keys to the flat like Christmas cards?"

She sat forward at that, but still out of the lamp's range, rubbing her cheek in a sudden despairing gesture. I wished I could see her expression as I added, "There are other things, too. Like the entry at the Registrar's. No one is just going to talk that away."

She shrugged. "Please believe me, Greg. I know it's a terrible thing to say, and how can I make you understand what I can't understand myself? Not completely, anyway." She drew a deep breath. "Look, the whole thing was a frightful mistake," and smiling thinly. "We would never have been happy together, you know."

"I'll bet!"

Ignoring that, she said, "Greg, can't we forget it, have the marriage annulled?" And then, very softly, as though knowing how thin the ice, "Uncle Hartley could arrange it – so that there's no scandal, no publicity."

"Annul our marriage! You must be out of your mind! Don't you realise that I love you? You loved me once, remember? Let's have a year together – two, three years – before we say it won't work. How can you or anyone else tell at this stage? Oh, Laurel, don't have doubts. I can make you happy – we were happy. Just give me a chance."

Her shrug was one of ruthless indifference, rejection of a merest triviality. "I'm sorry, Greg, I don't love you. Perhaps I did think so once, but I was wrong. So – I have no intention of being your wife – now or at any future time." She stood up, playing with the catch on the red handbag. "I thought you would be willing to save us all the scandal of publicity so soon – so soon after my mother's death." She paused, no doubt hoping that appeal to my better self would work. It didn't. "What good will it do you, anyway?" she asked coldly. "Or are you thinking the Sunday papers might be interested in your "Secret Marriage to Rowe's heiress?"

I could be nasty too. "Rowe's must be proud of you. You're a real chip off the old firm, aren't you? Following in the best family tradition of trampling everyone they couldn't buy into the dust."

"Fortunes aren't made on sentiment," she said sharply, drawing on her gloves, then added with a smile, "Please don't think too badly of me." And cajolingly, "Why not go back to Scotland and forget the whole thing? You're a handsome fellow, Greg. And you do have a certain charm when you're being kind. Oh, you'll meet someone else, I'm sure."

Angrily I sprang to the door and opened it. "If that's all you have to offer – a load of clichés – then go! Go now, before I forget myself and wallop your backside. You're a spoilt rich brat. You think you can buy and sell everything. Every man has his price! Well, I'm not for sale."

Oddly enough, instead of making her mad, she nodded eagerly. "Yes! You're quite right. That's just what I am – a spoilt rich brat. You go on remembering me like that and you'll be fine."

Remember her like that! I thought of the other Laurel I had loved, wondering where she hid in this ice cold creature. Wondering how I could ever reach her again. Angrily I took her in my arms and kissed her with nothing resembling the tenderness of love.

She didn't struggle as I thought she would, and for a few dizzy moments we were back at the beginning, the madness closing in again, as we clung together.

Then it was over. She struggled free and wiping the back of her hand across her mouth, she saw blood on it. Giving me a wild terrified look, she raced down the corridor. I watched her, thinking it's for ever this time.

But it wasn't quite for ever. Not quite yet.

Next morning, she telephoned, cautiously suggesting

59

lunch. "Please," she said when I sounded doubtful, wondering what little rack she was twisting me on today. "Please, Greg. It's – it's important."

The Rowe Arms was Rowe's concession to a family pub. Ye olde merrie England, and phoney as hell, from its Tudor rafters, its horse brasses (mass produced in Birmingham) to the electrically-driven candles, providing the Dickensian atmosphere of cheer and goodwill.

The lighting (one shrouded candle per table) was almost non-existent, and I practically needed radar to pick out Laurel, gloomily sitting at a corner table. My buoyant hopes faded, for even in that dim light, one look at her tragic face belied all hope of a lover's meeting. There was no beginning in store, merely an end.

Neither of us ate much and normal conversation had a way of falling apart at the seams. Finally, thrusting aside her coffee, she said, "I intended after last night to say many things – to save you from being hurt too much." She laughed shakily and looked round anxiously – as if someone listened. . . . "In the middle of a sleepless night, it's wonderful how the words come, how logical and simple it all sounds." In the gloom across the table, her face was infinitely sad. "Now it's all so trite, so useless."

"Don't bother to spare me. You're not coming back, is that it?"

"No, Greg. I'm not coming back. Not ever. But – "

"But what?"

Again that almost imperceptible nervy glance over her shoulder. The gloomy dining-room was almost deserted. "Get the check and we'll go," she said hastily.

In the dim cavern of an entrance hall, lit charmingly but inefficiently by coach lamps, she struggled into her coat. "Why don't you go away, Greg – now – today – just get on a train and – go," she whispered urgently. Her face and hair glowed pinkly in the unnatural light. It was flattering but couldn't conceal the hardness, the bitterness I had

60

noticed last night. Even the wraith-like beauty I had so admired had vanished and something coarser had taken its place.

God knows what tactics, what tortures, Rowe's had used to change her! Feeling pity, I said, "Come with me and we'll go together – right now."

She shook her head. A doll-like head of pink candyfloss. "No, Greg. I can't."

"Then why the devil did you bother to telephone? You made your point last night. Or were you needing the added satisfaction of tormenting me again?"

She put out a hand almost blindly. "No! No! I came – because – because – there's a limit to the things one can do. Even for money."

I stared at her. "What does money matter? We'll manage somehow. I'll get another job."

I had asked for it. The old treadmill again. She had never loved me. I was to go, there might be danger for me if I stayed – and persisted . . .

Outside, the fleeting sunshine had died. It was raining again. I followed her out, watching her tightening that damned ugly headscarf round her hair, pulling her coat collar up against the rain.

The anger . . . the shouting . . . the sight of her running towards me through the traffic. . . . the car. . . . the brakes screaming . . . "Vic, oh Vic" . . . Oh God, God help us!

And that was yesterday. A yesterday that has lasted a million years.

PART TWO

"Is it, in heav'n, a crime to love too well?"
(Pope)

CHAPTER ONE

The story of our sad little marriage might have doused its brief candle unseen with Laurel's death (and the will of Rowe's), but for a set of curious circumstances. The cussed streak in me which, once aroused, would never rest until it had touched the bottom of that barrel of lies.

Denials of marriage were one thing, but when bribery and house-breaking swiftly followed, it became a very fishy business indeed.

Two days after Laurel's death, there was a knock at the door. Three-quarters drunk (as was my normal condition between the hours of eight and eight when tinkering with the mural was impossible), I reeled over to the door. I expected Eva, full of missionary zeal.

It was Hartley Rowe, soberly attired in black suit and tie, as befitted the firm's most recent bereavement and – according to Eva – his umpteenth cousin! He was twisting the brim of his black homburg, in small, delicate, woman-like hands. The white face, with its melancholy triangles of eyes, was ludicrously that of the absent-minded clown arriving at a funeral, without first removing his circus make-up.

He took in my unshaven splendour, the crummy apartment and fast dwindling whisky bottle, with a kind of comradely tolerance, but firmly waved aside the proferred glass.

What the devil did he want? The mural was as finished as I could make it. There was no artistic touch left in the trembling hands, no inspiration in the soul that could only mourn for Laurel . . .

Rowe got straight to the point. "It's about Laurel. I thought we might have a little chat. As you apparently believe – er – that it was she you married, we – " he coughed – "the family, all realise how upset you must me. You mustn't think we're unsympathetic, you know." He darted a shrewd look at me, to see how I was taking it. "In the circumstances – " and there followed confused ambiguities washed down with soothing platitudes, all this verbiage dignifiedly in keeping with the great name of Rowe's.

Somewhere during this monologue, he started moving round the flat, eyes searching restlessly, picking up a book, examining a picture. My own eyes weren't focussing too well and I gave up trying to keep pace with him.

Suddenly he stopped, the flow of words dying like an old-fashioned gramophone run down. I was vaguely aware of a fat cheque being waved under my nose. The balm to soothe all wounds.

Again, that tiny apologetic cough. "You may, of course, use your own discretion about coming to the – er – funeral, but we – er – all hope you won't make any embarrassment for members of the family."

I examined the cheque. Five thousand pounds. "How much would I inherit, if I could prove Laurel was my wife?"

Calmly he named a sum, whose interest alone would have insured luxurious ease for the rest of my life, and added quietly, "If you can prove it."

"You can see the proof at the Registrar's in Weschester any time."

"Come now, you're not giving us credit for much sense, are you?" he said heavily. "Who were your witnesses? People from the firm? Friends of yours? Of Laurel's?"

I said they were a couple of passers-by and added defiantly. "They could be traced."

"Naturally. But you would be merely proving you had got married, not that you married Laurel Marsden-Smith. What was to stop you getting some girl with a superficial resemblance and having her pose as Laurel for the occasion?"

"She had her birth certificate. What about that?"

"Oh! Did you see it, by any chance?" I shook my head, remembering her difficulties (or so she said) of finding it without asking Mother, as it was only a copy of the original which had been lost long ago. Oh, Laurel!

Rowe's calm, "Birth certificates have been forged before today," was a mere echo of my own thoughts. "None of this would be difficult for a determined blackmailer." He paused. "Tell me, can you honestly imagine Laurel Marsden-Smith with all she had, getting married in this hole-in-the-corner fashion?"

I couldn't. "It was her idea. Her mother was ill – "

"Yes, yes," he said impatiently. "I heard your story and I also heard hers. That she had never seen you before until the day you arrived and claimed she was your wife."

I thought rapidly. "What about her signature at the Registrar's?"

He was prepared for that too. "You realise we have nothing formal, she would not sign any official document for the firm until she reached twenty-five. Of course, there are personal letters to various people, myself included. Birthday cards, postcards – that sort of thing." He let it sink in. "However, MacGregor, at Rowe's we never condemn a man without a fair hearing. We'll go to the Registrar's and settle this whole thing for once and for all. Shall we say nine-thirty tomorrow morning?" he asked pleasantly.

I should have known by his easy manner that he had

the whole thing nicely tied up long before I stepped into the Rolls. I sat down beside a large stolid man, wearing a bland expression and a burlesque edition of a belted trenchcoat and felt hat that I thought the I.R.A. and M.I.5 had taken copyright on long ago! The combination fairly shrieked policeman!

"This is Inspector Wiggs, MacGregor," said Rowe amiably. "I think you'll agree that it is as well to have a reliable witness."

It looked like being an uncomfortable journey, with the Inspector silently chewing the ends of his luxuriant moustache. Rowe's face had an air of quiet triumph.

"Had much crime recently, Inspector?" he asked suddenly.

Wiggs stopped chewing. "Nothing startling, you know," and eyeing me sternly, "People here behave themselves, MacGregor."

Rowe chuckled, rubbing his white hands together. "They do indeed! And we intend to keep it that way, don't we, Inspector?" There was a pause. "Let me see, when *was* our last big crime?"

Wiggs replied instantly. "Three years next month. A nasty hit-and-run road accident." He looked out of the window, adding bitterly, "With some suspicions of foul play."

"You never did find anyone for it, did you?" enquired Rowe pleasantly. He was obviously enjoying himself.

Wiggs scowled and I got a queer feeling of cat-and-mouse, of there being more behind this innocent conversation than the words implied. Wiggs was saying, "We didn't get anyone then, but who knows – maybe tomorrow, or next week – even next year, some fresh evidence will come to light," he shrugged. "Then, we'll start again." And I could see him, too, plodding the pavements, relentlessly tracking down his prey.

At the Registrar's, the entry was duly checked with the

signature of Laurel Marsden-Smith and, as I had already guessed, it bore not the slightest resemblance.

Wiggs grunted and delivered me a nasty little caution about blackmailing. "If I had my way, I would put you inside for a spell. You can thank Mr. Rowe and his goodness of heart that you're not behind bars."

"No, no," said Rowe, at his most fatherly, "we can't have that, Inspector. It seems that someone played a rather cruel joke on poor MacGregor. After all, he has done some valuable work for us. Besides, think of the scandal if we had him put in prison. It would never do." And the scorned cheque was once more being waved under my nose. "Maybe you'll accept this now, MacGregor. I can assure you it's quite normal procedure with Rowe's." He smiled at Wiggs. "When we're very satisfied with a piece of work, like the mural, we usually add a little bonus at the end of it. I hope poor MacGregor hasn't been finding himself in financial difficulties, since the painting has taken longer than we thought." He turned and said reproachfully. "I like you, MacGregor, you're a good worker. In the normal way, you would have been kept in our employment, doing little jobs." (My mind boggled!) "However, in the circumstances – " His shrug indicated regretful dismissal.

"Much more than you deserve, I'd say, young fellow," said Wiggs, now fairly worrying his moustache. More indeed! Even the seemingly suspicious business of being offered hush money had turned itself into a nice "little bonus."

Rowe folded the cheque and tucked it into my breast pocket, patted it with a nicely calculated paternal gesture, whilst Wiggs disgustedly watched, as if he'd like to run me in, or personally push me back under my stone.

Then someone made a fatal mistake.

CHAPTER TWO

Feeling crushed and defeated, that I could hardly wait to leave Rowe's Vale for ever, with its memories all gone sour, I went back to the flat and found that someone, none too subtly, had given it a pretty thorough going-over.

Police? Remembering Wiggs, I wondered, then concluded that it was unlikely. In the words of that hoary old gangsterism – "they had nothing on me!"

Uncle Hartley? A likelier bet. But why? The odd thing was that with few exceptions, everything had been neatly replaced. There was nothing missing. Not that I had anything worth the stealing, but there's an unpleasant vulnerability about the feeling that one's possessions have been thoroughly searched.

Particularly after being craftily lured away so that the job could be done in comparative safety!

To go to the good Inspector with this lack of evidence brought an ominous feeling that the next stop would be a good psychiatrist (at the instigation, no doubt, of Rowe's nicely blended sweetness and light.) Even I could recognise the makings of a fine persecution complex.

Well, they weren't getting rid of me as easily as that. Here was something to work on at last. There could be only one reason for that search!

Someone had left a loose end – a loophole which would prove I had spoken the truth!

All I had to do was to find it first. Of course, it would have been a great help to know *what* I was looking for!

Carefully cleaning and packing my paint brushes, a

picture formed itself of Laurel sitting here that last evening, wearing the hideous headscarf in shades of purple madder, one of the few colours I could hardly bring myself to use. Certainly the intruder had used her key to the flat, for there was not a single mark of violent entry anywhere. He could hardly have shinned up four floors of sheer brick, and the fire escape merely led into the outside corridor.

Following on from there – there was someone, now in possession of Laurel's key who *knew* I was speaking the truth. Was the search then merely a precaution, *in case* I had other evidence? In case Laurel had been careless?

My subsequent whisky lunch brought a mood of defiance. I decided to attend the funeral of Laurel Marsden-Smith – "family only and no flowers". It wouldn't do me any good, I knew that, but it was my undisputed right as her widower. The other reason was that it would certainly nettle Uncle Hartley.

I located the crematorium with difficulty. Camouflaged in park and upper income-group suburbia, it was a rather arch building masquerading as an ivy-covered chapel of Pre-Raphaelite splendour, suggesting "The Light of the World" rather than the jet-age-space-theme dear to Rowe's buildings – all precarious angles and unpleasantly eager for orbit! Aye, there was a lesson for the moralist somewhere . . .

There were fewer cars than one would have expected even for a private funeral, with the depressing assumption that Laurel, lonely and friendless for most of her life, was leaving it in the same sad condition.

The service had begun and slipping inside the chapel, defiantly ignoring the stares and whispers, I hurried down to the front.

There, listening respectfully to the prayers for the deceased, I got a prickly sensation of something wrong, and found to my horror that this was the funeral of a complete stranger.

The woman in deep black, weeping unrestrainedly alongside, became unmistakeably the widow, whilst the close relatives, bewildered, indignant, whispered questions about my presence. I fled.

Presumably, I had agitatedly misread the press notice, and completely unnerved at the prospect of going through it all again, I hurried outside, wondering where Laurel lay, with only a few moments left on earth. Suddenly I desperately longed to say farewell to her.

It was a day in keeping with sorrow, with little warmth or movement in the frozen autumn sunshine. In the garden of memory, the roses had long since perished and only yews, coarse, dark and implicitly funereal, remained.

As I stood undecided, from somewhere nearby came the faint sound of a typewriter. Thoughtfully noting its general location, I went back into the building and down a long corridor found a door marked "Office."

The girl behind the desk was young and pretty, her smile innocently radiant. Then noticing sombre suit and black tie, she gulped it back with an apologetic blush. Embarrassment and youth suggested she was new to the job. It was better than I had dared hope, providing a unique advantage in her probable ignorance of any strict etiquette involved.

I became a bereaved cousin and listening sympathetically, she said, "Oh, yes. It'll be all right to wait." Back past the chapel we went, into a small room about whose sober hangings, discreet furniture, and tastefully arranged flowers, there hung the implacable, eradicable smell of death.

The girl looked at her watch. "Will you wait? It's more than half-an-hour until – "

"Has the coffin been closed?" I asked.

She looked nervous. "Well, the men – they're busy –

with – er, next door," and her nod indicated the general direction of the chapel.

For a moment, my heart sank, then taking pity on me, she smiled. "Oh, seeing you're one of the family, and coming so far, I expect it'll be all right. You go ahead."

She rushed out, Taking a deep breath, I lifted the lid of the coffin.

CHAPTER THREE

The bus was far past Rowe's Vale, past Tom's valley, out and away into the clean open country, before I could gather my wits.

I had seen death overtake the old many times, but never anyone as young as Laurel. I was totally unprepared for the terrible change that death could make, the hand that wiped away from a young and lovely face, every vestige of personality, leaving it a blank sheet.

For poor Laurel, there was not even dignity left. I had not realised there would be bruises still, purplish ugly marks down one side of her face, indelible – for ever – where presumably she had struck the ground that fatal afternoon.

Where was my love, my Laurel, vital and laughing? Not the girl who lay there, ugly, broken, her lies stilled for ever.

That evening, still horribly shaken, I discovered the reason why Hartley Rowe had the flat searched. In a more appreciative frame of mind, I would have recognised it as a lucky break. The first unravelling of the skein.

Eva came round, her booming manner suspiciously casual, darting anxious sidelong glances, as if I were suffering from some strange malady where one wrong word might hurl me over the precipice. She dumped down the huge basket, rummaged amongst the clatter of knitting needles, tangled wool and unpaid bills to surface with the local newspaper, folded at the story of Laurel's funeral.

"You were wise to stay away, Greg, it really was most upsetting." And shaking her head sadly I imagined her there, whispering to Hartley Rowe. Watching, waiting, craning her neck – ready to support me should I fail . . .

Angrily I rolled the newspaper and thrust it back into the basket. It landed beside an object which seemed vaguely familiar.

A small bright red handbag. Laurel's!

"Where did you get this?"

Eva shrugged guiltily. "Surely you remember, Greg. She dropped it – that afternoon – when – when – "

"All right, all right. Give it to me."

She hesitated, brown eyes wobbling dangerously. "I can't do that!" she said in outraged tones, as if I had asked her to steal sweeties from the school tuck shop, or profane the Girl Guide's Law. "It's for Mr. Rowe," she said virtuously, "I intended giving it to him this afternoon, but well, it wasn't an opportune time."

"Why the devil have you kept it this long? You see the man every day."

There was a look of bovine reproach in the round eyes. "Don't be so mean, Greg. I didn't know I had it. What I mean is, when I picked it up with the gloves – they're inside, I – er – didn't know she was going to . . . I was just holding them, that's all."

I remembered Eva standing there, bag and gloves in hand, in the rain. It seemed like a long, long time ago.

She sighed enormously. "I put them in the basket, I remember, because they were getting so wet. Then you were in such a state. I needed all my energies and thoughts to cope with you."

"No one asked you to," I said ungratefully.

Ignoring that, she continued. "Well, I forgot and they got covered with my own things, until I was looking for something last night." She laughed. "I was so surprised! Couldn't think where they had come from. Greg! You

aren't – surely you aren't going to *look* inside! Greg!"
Her shocked voice ebbed on a shriek of protest.

Still playing with the catch, I weighed the bag in
my hand. "What difference would it make to Laurel
now? Don't worry, I'll see it gets to Mr. Rowe. Goodbye, Eva."

Dubiously watching, reluctant to abandon Laurel's
property, she asked anxiously, "Can't I make you some
coffee or something?"

"No, thanks, I'm busy packing." (I'd have to be brusque
to get rid of her). "He packs fastest who packs alone, you
know!"

"All right, no need to be surly. I can take a hint!" And
biting her lips nervously, she touched the whisky bottle.
"You've been at that again, I see. It doesn't do any
good, you know. Just makes you unpleasantly aggressive,
that's all."

After she had gone, I sat looking at the handbag, feeling
like a new man. Gone was the helplessness of wondering
whether I might have had a brainstorm, whether I was
really a head-case!

One thing was abundantly clear since Eva related the
bag's history:

Rowe would naturally suppose that I had it, knowing I
was with her at the end. Supposing that its return was
vital? Supposing that Laurel had kept something indiscreet
– marriage lines, for instance, or the wedding ring she had
kissed and deposited in her purse that last afternoon in
London? Perhaps one of the many, many letters I had
written to her *poste restante* afterwards.

What more obvious place to keep any, or all, of these
indiscreet treasures, than in her handbag?

Confidently I emptied the contents on the table.

What a bitter disappointment! There was nothing.
Nothing but the mundane things most women carry.

A pair of gloves the colour of terracotta. I remembered

76

her twisting them in her hands at the table in the Rowe Arms that last day. Make-up in a *pouchette*, powder compact, comb, dark glasses, and a purse.

There was a key-ring bearing two keys. A worn Yale, yellow-tagged with the number "25". A smaller ornate key – somehow familiar.

I tried the purse next. There was no wedding ring, only a ten pound note and a few coins. Angrily thrusting the money back, my hand encountered two small pieces of folded paper.

A left luggage ticket, from Weschester Station, date-stamped October 21st, and a page torn from a notebook, with "V.B.421" scribbled on it. Her hairdresser or dentist? Someone she'd met and promised to contact?

Well, Rowe hardly needed risk a break-in for this lot of meaningless rubbish. He could have it tomorrow, delivered personally!

I sat back in my chair. Why the devil hadn't he just come right out and asked for it? Why all the stealth? The conclusion was obvious.

Something was not as trivial as it looked!

In retrospect, even Rowe's apparent innocent roving of the flat, whilst he tried to persuade me to accept the cheque, now seemed sinister. And how ironic that, as he anxiously planned to have the flat burgled, the reason for it was there under his very nose – in Eva's shopper, which he doubtless tripped over and cursed quite regularly. I laughed – so close and all unknowing.

What did Rowe *know* the bag contained? And taking my time, I examined it minutely. It was soft leather, unlined, so that did not take long. The make-up, gloves, glasses and comb seemed straight-forward enough, also the purse with its money.

What had I left?

A Left Luggage ticket.

The words "V.B.421" on a scrap of paper.
Two keys: A worn Yale, numbered "25" on a yellow tag, and . . .

I gave a cry of triumph. No wonder the other key looked familiar. And checking with my key-ring, it was undoubtedly the *duplicate* key for the suitcase I had lent Laurel in London.

Something on that Left Luggage ticket rang a bell too . . .

The date: October 21st!

Now there was a day I wouldn't forget in a hurry. And neither would Laurel. The day which began my forlorn vigil in Edinburgh. The fateful day on which her mother fell out of the train!

CHAPTER FOUR

Long after I laid the ticket aside, the date October 21st came springing back to torment me. For a moment, I toyed with the fantastic idea that there might be some connection between ticket and suitcase key – that it *was* my suitcase in the Left Luggage!

I saw Laurel taking it to London out of momentary sentiment, then in the horror of her mother's death, guiltily abandoning it in a kind of superstitious terror. Still, that seemed a bit tortuous when presumably she would be met with a car at the station. It would have been easier to have just left it unclaimed on the train!

Well, my disillusions did not allow for sentiment. If it was my suitcase, I needed it. Beside being Callum's birthday present to me, and each time he saw it, he lovingly told me how much it had cost him, etc., I could imagine his fury if I appeared home without it again. Anyway, it was an easy matter to check at the Station.

It was now Tuesday. The unveiling of the mural was scheduled for Friday – a date fixed months ago, now alas, after some hasty finishing touches, the paint would hardly be dry.

By the weekend, I would be thankfully quit of Rowe's Vale. Skipping the unveiling was most tempting, but in some curious way, I felt being present reasserted my innocence of any duplicity.

There was another stronger reason too. I was eager to meet the mysterious Vic, whom Laurel had loved. And if – as I suspected – he was connected with Rowe's, in all probability he would be there. I relished the chance of settling a number of scores with him Not only for usurping me with Laurel, but I was pretty sure he was my burglar too.

I doubted, like all the late starters who fall so deeply in love, that I would ever love again. Perhaps the day would dawn when the memory of Laurel could be faced without pain, with philosophical cynicism as "I loved a girl once . . ." Perhaps this persistent inner voice would fade. The voice that whispered of something terribly wrong, something vital in its urgency, that impelled me to go on searching.

Searching is fine if you know what you're looking for, of course, but at this stage it was merely a bone in the throat of my subconscious memory.

On top of my own troubles, there was the forlorn business of getting Tom Markham out of the valley and established somewhere else before the opening of the dam. The day of the flooding grew ominously nearer and Tom's ineffectual ostrich manner fairly smacked of senility.

Curiously enough, Eva, whose heart regularly bled for lonely young men, while probable lost dogs turned her into a quivering amorphous mass, was singularly unsympathetic about poor old Tom.

"Why bother about that tiresome old man, Greg? Everyone at Rowe's knows *him*." She groaned. "Always complaining about something or other, and Mr. Rowe has been so wonderful to the old people. I can't imagine why anyone should want to stay in that dreary damp valley, all alone, when there's such a lovely old folks' home. He must be barmy! I bet he doesn't even have a bathroom."

Sharply retorting that I had lived in a croft with no bathroom and only an outside closet most of my life, without undue suffering, Eva shook her head, somewhat mollified. "But I do think he should at least be grateful," she said lamely. "I do wish I could come and help you clear up the flat, Greg," (as if I had asked her!) and pointing to a stack of ledgers, she gave a weary sigh. "There's so much to do. Auditors coming, estate still to settle – ."

"Who gets the money now?" I asked calmly enough. Laurel's vast fortune had never seemed sufficiently real to interest me.

"It'll go into the firm mostly – except for one or two bequests." Briskly she changed the subject. "Are you staying for the opening of the dam? Royal visits are always so exciting! Just think, they'll probably come and look at your mural, too." No use explaining to Eva that my interest in Royalty ended with Bonnie Prince Charlie and the battlefield of Culloden. I said I couldn't promise to stay that long and got the address of the Housing Section.

They had nothing for Tom, as a single man, except a room in the Old Folk's Home. Finally, by taking full responsibility and paying the rent in advance, I secured the flat for him until the tenant's return.

When I told him, he just hunched his shoulders and looked more like a dejected lizard than ever. Then waving his hand round the cluttered room, he said, "What about all this? I can't leave my things. Will there be room for them?"

So, on the morning of the mural's debut, after a great deal of argument, persuasion and suspicions (darkly directed at the furniture men who had a terrible time getting the van back up that shocking road), Tom was moved into the flat. His large furniture went into store, the small valuables came with him. We left the house, naked and empty but for one broken-down chair. "Only fit for firewood," said Tom.

It took just a few minutes for the flat's repellent modernity to change into something resembling a junk room at the back of the British Museum and character was swiftly acquired from stuffed birds and blunderbuss, the latter parked menacingly behind the door!

However, it was only a ghost who came to live in the flat. The vibrant spirited personality was left behind to briefly haunt the empty house in the valley. At the time, I was brash enough to consider his behaviour perfectly normal, especially for an old man nearing ninety, who had just had his lifetime's roots uplifted!

Self-righteously pretending I had done my best by Tom, I went to the ceremony in the canteen. It looked particularly attractive today, mostly due to curtains being drawn over the mural! Pity they hadn't saved their prize money and invested in a good pair of curtains instead, I thought, sipping indifferent sherry and watching the cocktail hour move fiendishly under way.

The extravagently competitive wear of the ladies was matched by the extravagant competitive speeches from the men. Mr. Rowe treated me to a misty-eyed concern, that aroused suspicions of too many cocktails, a twinge of uneasy conscience, or both.

In the distance I glimpsed Frosty Voice, violently and expensively hatted, and Dr. Fellton bowed gravely as he reared his great head in the direction of the sherries.

Eva was there too, insecurely contained in a sheath dress and grimly clinging to my arm like a wardress with a particularly slippy prisoner. She fed me on cigarettes and savouries cooing with loud, proud delight over the mural when the curtains were removed.

Candidly eyeing heroic workers and glamourous vignettes of purely mythical Rowes, seeing anew glaring faults and impossibilities, and wondering why everyone else didn't too, I listened with an air of detachment to the praises of "this brilliant young man". Who was he? Certainly not myself, remembering the hacking, the scraping, the dullness of it all. Had some other character stood up and acknowledged the applause, I wouldn't have been surprised. I would have clapped like mad.

Then came the small purgatory of all cocktail parties. Sherry finished, sandwiches curling, canapés frankly repulsive. Watches were consulted both furtively and frequently. A sigh of weariness, too early for dinner, too late to do anything. Smiles grew glazed and yawns escaped unstifled. What a bore! Whispers of "How soon can we get away, dear?"

I said to Eva, "I'm going." She looked disappointed, enjoying to the full, the reflection of my moment of glory. "We must say goodbye to Mrs. Rowe first, Greg."

"I haven't said hello to her yet!" Which of the overdressed females could be the wife of Mr. Rowe's bosom?

"She's over there," said Eva. Back towards us, she was deep in conversation with a dear old lady from whose flower-bedecked hat, roses nodded agreement with the hostess's every remark.

Getting round the near side of Mrs. Rowe, I stepped back. No wonder she hadn't bounded over to meet me.

Mrs. Rowe was Aunt Judith – Frosty Voice herself!

CHAPTER FIVE

I was all for slipping silently away and it seemed unlikely that my absence would be either noted or mourned. Then there was some pushing and a yell as someone spilt something or got stepped on, which distracted the two ladies *tête-a-tête* and Mrs. Rowe and I faced each other.

A small pink glow moved upwards from her neck and the friend seizing a chance of escape, leaned over, pecking her cheek: "I really must fly, darling . . ."

Looking absent-minded, Mrs. Rowe patted her arm and murmured, "Don't worry about it, dear, I'll have a chat with Vic."

I swung round angrily. Vic – here?

He must be: With that family set-up, it had to be the same Vic whose name Laurel died proclaiming.

Mrs. Rowe and I shook hands with such mutual distaste that we could scarcely refrain from wiping our hands down our jackets afterwards. I watched Eva gushing at Mrs. Rowe, then abruptly I interrupted, with: "How's Vic, Mrs. Rowe?"

"I have no idea who you're talking about," she said coldly.

"I asked after Vic." Eva was twigging urgently at my arm and momentarily the cold face of Mrs. Rowe was transformed. A great smile severed the enamel.

"Well, hello, darling," she shrieked, "so good to see you!" But not to me. A bejewelled, bedizzened female was spewed out of the crowd to land beside us. I felt that Mrs. Rowe's exit with this puffing creature was just a shade sharp for good manners.

Eva was muttering, "What was all that about? Don't you think you're sometimes rather rude?"

"I'm just interested at the moment, Eva. I can be a lot ruder! Know anyone called Vic? Think hard! What does she call Rowe, for instance?"

"She calls *Mr.* Rowe 'Hartley'," Eva said with dignity. "I've told you before, I don't know anyone called Vic. Who mentioned him anyway?"

"Mrs. Rowe did. You must have heard her, when she was saying goodbye to her chum."

Eva stared. "Are you sure?"

"Of course I'm sure!"

"Greg, I certainly didn't hear her say anything about Vic. You could be mistaken." she studied me carefully. "How can you possibly be certain what you heard in a throng like that?" And as we went over to the car park, "Aren't you getting an obsession with this Vic idea?"

We argued right to Weschester Central station where Eva had insisted taxi-ing my packed luggage, to be sent home in advance. With Tom and his possessions, space in the flat was rather limited.

Right at the other side of the station, tucked away depressingly far from the platforms, was the Left Luggage Office. I said to Eva, "Just a minute, there's something I want over there."

There was no doubt about it, the suitcase I obtained on the ticket from Laurel's purse was my own!

Eva waited at the car. "When did you leave that?" she asked.

"I didn't leave it. Laurel put it there."

"Laurel?" she demanded sharply, then with a long-suffering sigh clearly indicating "There he goes again!" she unlocked the boot.

"But it feels empty, Greg!" she said, giving it an

admonitory shake. "Why on earth leave an empty suit-case?"

I couldn't answer that, either, and letting in the clutch, Eva smiled indulgently. "Greg, it wasn't really Laurel, was it? You're – you're just trying to make me angry again, aren't you?"

"Oh, forget it, Eva!"

She still sounded rather offended when we said good-night at the flat.

Tom sat by the electric fire moping miserably. After an unequal battle at cheering him, I went to bed depressed with everything and everyone, rapidly embracing Eva's views that Tom might at least be grateful. It wasn't my fault. Yet, yet – we were all of us guilty, and the pathetic story of the very old like the poor was "ever with us."

I picked up the suitcase to thrust it into the cupboard. And as I did so, something slithered inside.

Curious now, I unlocked it, expecting to find some overlooked garment of Laurel's.

What I did find was astonishing in its sheer absurdity.

A station porter's jacket and cap. Navy blue, thinnish material and well worn at that.

There must be some mistake! I sat there laughing with the things in my hands. What on earth were they doing in Laurel's suitcase? A fancy dress ball, perhaps? Hardly! Holding up the jacket, I knew it had never fitted Laurel. It was made for a large man, about my height but considerably broader.

Angry and mystified, I threw them back into the suitcase and got out Laurel's handbag, to pour over the contents again, like a miser with his hoard.

I looked at that scrap of paper again. V.B.421.

What did it signify. A telephone number? With V.B. perhaps the person's initials?

My heart began to beat wildly. "V for Victor", of course!

An hour later, searching methodically through the telephone directory, I found:

"V. Barnes, 139 Sycamore Grove. Telephone no. Rowe's Vale 421."

The missing Vic. It must be!

CHAPTER SIX

I dialled the number several times, but it rang unanswered. I looked at my watch. It was after ten and too late to go searching for Sycamore Grove. Presumably, Victor had a keen social life!

However, early next morning, I was on the bus, with the upper deck to myself but for a man crouched behind a newspaper on the back seat. Buses passed us, dripping with passengers, in the direction of Rowe's Vale.

This was my first visit to the red-brick suburbia, and its serried ranks of houses were so depressingly alike, that we seemed to be going round in circles. Suddenly I doubted if this was the right bus. "Is this right for Sycamore Grove?" I asked the man behind the newspaper, but either deaf or asleep, he ignored me.

Hastening downstairs, the conductor doused a cigarette neatly and sprang to the bell. "Sycamore Grove? Next stop, sir!"

Two minutes later I stood at the gate of No. 139.

The whole journey had been something of a surprise, and Victor Barnes' residence kept up the tone. Out-of-season polythene flowers bloomed lavishly but dustily in the front window of a sad dispirited semi-detached, beyond a tiny patch of ground that had given up all pretence to be a garden long ago. It was hardly the flashy establishment I had imagined for Laurel's mysterious lover.

The surprises weren't over yet. The door was opened by a small, bald-headed man, of indeterminate age. "Ay,

Ah'm Barnes, lad," he said in a pronounced Yorkshire accent, showing a mouthful of black decaying teeth.

The suspicion I had on the bus that the theory was wrong, grew stronger. Feeling miserable, I muttered a story about being a freelance child photographer . . .

The Victor I had imagined, the Great Casanova himself, would have laughed, tipped a wink, said sorry he wasn't married. The man before me took out steel-rimmed glasses, polished them, wrinkled his nose to keep them secure and said meekly: "Half a mo', Ah'll get t'wife."

After a background of mutinous murmurings, the wife appeared. She was almost beaten into the ground by the sheer weight of armoury in her hair and carried a half-dressed struggling baby, whilst thumb-sucking, wide-eyed twin girls peered round her skirts.

She looked frankly hostile and said shortly. "We had a fellow from Dorian's last week. Remember, Vince? You're not from there, are you?" Groaning at the name "Vince", I gave an honest no.

"We're just back from my sister's wedding and we can't afford any more pictures," she said frankly. "You would be wasting your time, mister."

That was a relief! Always handling a sketch book with more dexterity than a camera, I regarded the latter with great awe. In fact, even the unsophisticated Box Brownie, won in a painting competition when I was ten, could be relied upon to decapitate humans and turn innocent church spires into earthquake victims.

"Sorry, lad," said Mr. Barnes, "Some other time, perhaps."

Mrs. Barnes relented. "Ay, call next time you come by."

Her husband eyed her with unmistakeable pride and devotion: "That's a good idea, lass."

I had a last despairing try. "Haven't I seen you somewhere before, Mr. Barnes?"

He looked surprised and interested, but certainly not guilty. "Ah don't think so."

"Expect you're at Rowe's – I was taking pictures there the other day."

He laughed. "You'd be hard placed to find anyone hereabouts who isn't with Rowe's!" And smiling broadly, "Ah work there all right, but you wouldn't likely see me. Look after t'office boilers!"

I tried again. "Pity the daughter having that accident, wasn't it?"

Mrs. Barnes clucked sadly. "So young and pretty, she was."

"Was she?" I asked indifferently. "Did you see her much?" I asked Barnes, risking sounding like a sensation-hunter.

He shook his head. "Not since she was a little lass. They had some alterations to their kitchen and she was always there watching me. A lonely kid, glad of someone to talk to in that great big house. We got real pally, she used to call me Barney," he paused and blinked his eyes sadly. "That poor little rich girl angle seemed clean daft till I saw t'life she had. Someone had tried to kidnap her once – it was quite a sensation – and since then t'poor mite had lived like a prisoner, abroad most of t'time, so she even spoke English a bit like one of those foreign kids. Aye, it's a bad business. She never did have much life one way and another." He leaned over and chucked the baby under the chin. "Ah hope our three do a lot better, even without their Dad being a millionaire."

Feeling hypocritical and unpleasantly mealy-mouthed, I said goodbye.

The flat was empty. Tom invariably disappeared after breakfast. Where he spent his days wasn't my business, but I was pretty sure he went back to his valley and walked among its ghosts in the empty echoing house.

As I finished packing, this queer feeling of urgency returned, the feeling that my feet were anchored to this hated place by invisible chains. Yet without the mural, and nothing but the wounds Laurel had left me to lick, even I could see the dangers of morbid obsession with a girl who was dead, and had practically wrecked my life with her cheating and her lies.

Why stay? Why not clear out, turn cynical and at least, learn something from the bitter experience?

Why stay for a wordless voice nagging deep inside, of the formless memory of things seen, and recognised as hopelessly wrong?

CHAPTER SEVEN

Idly, I took up the telephone directory again. Perhaps I was wrong – perhaps "V.B.421" was a dress pattern, something written down and (remembering Eva!) forgotten about long ago.

The first page was open at the dialling instructions, underneath, a map of the area with its various exchanges.

Wearily I started at letter "A".

By the time I had reached "D", my eyes were going together. As good clean family reading, the telephone directory may have something, but as a dramatic story, it'll never make the best-seller class.

Then, quite suddenly, I found it. Someone in the "D's," with a number on the *Vansett Bridge exchange*!

V.B., of course! A place not a person's name. My preoccupation with Vic had been blinding me to that.

Triumphantly, I dialled the number and waited. There was a click at the other end and a business-like female said, "Vansett Bridge 421. Can I help you?"

"May I speak to Victor please?"

"Victor? Victor who? What is his other name?"

"I don't know."

"A moment please." A pause and the rustle of paper. "Has he been with us long? I don't see any name Victor on our lists." Another pause. "Are you sure you have the right number, caller?"

"You are Vansett Bridge 421?"

"Yes! The Rowe Vale Private Clinic."

Hastily apologising, I rang off.

Rowe Vale Private Clinic! I remembered its beautiful setting and Laurel saying that the County Council had run it at a loss as a mental home. Now Rowe's owned most of it as a quiet rest-home for voluntary patients. The way I was going, I should have rang back and booked myself a room!

Angrily, I decided I was wasting my time. Presumably Laurel knew someone at the Clinic, and had perhaps promised her mother to enquire after them. If she were anything like Eva, the note had lain forgotten in her purse for months.

Determined to be sensible, save that I was putting far too much stress on my "feeling" about Laurel, I was all set to get the train next day when two letters arrived. One was from the art gallery in London said my paintings had arrived. Would I pay them a visit to go through the pictures and arrange the cataloguing and pricing? On their journey from Scotland these details had gone astray.

The other letter, also postmarked London, was in brother Callum's sprawling hand. He and Sandy Mac (his bachelor farmer chum from the next village) were on holiday – it was the quiet time on the croft. "We thought to drop by so that we could all travel North together." He added wistfully, "Maybe we could get a wee look at that grand painting, too."

For the Royal "We", substitute "I". Sandy Mac and I had no time for one another. I still smarted from his merciless bullying years ago, inciting the older boys to "knock the life out o' that daft brither o' Callum's." There was no real animosity, just the instinct of the hencoop to peck to death their weakest member!

By going up to London tomorrow, I could make it back in time for Callum. Even a day away would be a blessed relief. Certainly, if I stayed here with nothing to keep me occupied much longer, I'd drive myself daft!

In case I had another uninvited caller during Tom's daily absences, (using Laurel's key to the flat), I took with me the suitcase, the porter's suit – and just to be spiteful, Laurel's red handbag!

CHAPTER EIGHT

London is many things to many men. All it brought me was a curious sense of annihilation and, merging with its crowded streets, a Zombie-like loss of identity. This impersonal atmosphere was stronger in reality than merely sitting watching London on film, where at least someone commented, however facetiously.

Now, not even the sight of my own feet on the pavements, or my tall gaunt reflection peering out of shop windows and fancy mirrors, was reassuring. I was a ghost – the ghost of myself without Laurel, empty and sadly futile.

My dejected spirits didn't exactly soar when I reached the "Treasure Trove" and arranged the exhibition details with the proprietor's assistant, a giggling little man with heavily permed hair, who fussed, fluttered his long red eyelashes, stank of perfume, and called everyone – including me – "Darling!"

The gallery was housed in one of those fashionably old world squares right in the heart of London, where the rumble of a stagecoach remains forever just a breath away. It looked as if a benevolent time – to say nothing of Hitler's bombs – had tiptoed gently past and let it sleep undisturbed.

Opposite was a tiny park, dusty perhaps, but full of ancient well-meaning trees and irreverent extrovert sparrows. Over the treetops, the skyscrapers of new London peeped, an intrusion from another world, a race of gigantic robots, looming larger and stealthily nearer. One day the trees would grind under their weight, and the sparrows cheep no more.

I remembered that Laurel's friend, Lorna Blagdon, lived quite near. Memories of Laurel preparing to visit her that honeymoon afternoon, and my jealous displeasure, brought a futile wave of longing. I could see her so clearly and London would be forever associated with that brief fleeting happiness. She had certainly left an eradicable mark on my life, with nothing she had not touched and claimed as her own.

The pain was so great that I decided to go and see Lorna Blagdon, to find consolation in talking to someone who had also loved Laurel. Perhaps I had judged Lorna hastily. Anyway, even if she didn't have a heart of gold, probably like most women, she was sentimental about the past.

She would weep and tell me small endearing things about her friendship with Laurel and I would feel uplifted and sustained by this common bond between us.

My hand was on the receiver in the telephone kiosk, when I decided not to call. If she didn't already know, how would she take Laurel's death over the telephone? No, it was too brutal, with Gateside Circle only five minutes walk away.

(I was lying to myself again. Curious to meet Lorna, what if we had nothing to say to another over the telephone? What if she didn't invite me round?)

Gateside Circle consisted of flat-faced three-storied Victorian terrace houses, once demure behind railings, with their stone-flighted entrances, but the railings had blasted out of guns long ago, and the charms of door-knocker and shoe-scraper had vanished when, after the war, the houses had been transformed into private hotels or flats.

Such was No. 25. Tired, seedy yellow brick outside and on the inside, long narrow corridors and unlovely staircases, which I suspected, were designed on economic grounds. In a more spacious age, such tortuous access would have seemed claustrophobic.

Someone hadn't spared the paint either. I'm not mad about gravy brown but I winced painfully at a door painted yellow ochre and purple madder, and heard Laurel's ghost whisper: "Lorna's colour-blind, you know!" She must be, I thought, seeing her name "L. Blagdon" above the bell, not to get heart failure from an eye-shatterer like that.

I rang the bell twice. There was no answer and cursing myself for not telephoning in the first place, I took a bus back to Piccadilly, arranged for some extra frames, then tried Lorna's number again.

It was six o'clock. The last train to Rowe's Vale was at eight, and I wanted to be on it. Pretending the telephone was out of order, I went back to Gateside Circle. Once more I rang the bell.

I knew it wouldn't be any use.

I was just leaving when an elderly woman wearing a lacy beehive hat, *très élégante*, and never meant for the large red-bad-tempered face beneath it, stared round the banisters.

"You here again, young man?" she demanded sharply. Somewhat lamely I conceded that I was and she said, "No use you trying her door. She hasn't been here for weeks now." She paused, taking in my height and large feet, before asking suspiciously (and just a thought hopefully), "You from the police?"

I laughed. "No! Just a friend."

She curled her lip, clearly indicating the sort of "friend" she took me to be! And clearly disappointed that I wasn't from the police she snapped, "Well, she's not here and don't ask me where she's gone. Touring, I expect!" Her harsh, unpleasant shout of laughter gave the word a vivid implication of "whoring!"

"Rent's paid up to the end of the month, so if she's not

97

back then, it's good riddance. Plenty of respectable people would be glad of the apartment."

A couple of them trudged upstairs, new clothes and hand luggage plus nervous giggles, clearly proclaiming honeymooners.

The beehive hat melted into butter. "Oh, here you are! I've been waiting for you." There was an apologetic mumble about missing a train. "Well, it doesn't matter, does it, now you're here?" (Could it be the same shrew?) "Last door on the left. Here's the key, I hope you'll be happy with us."

Murmuring thanks, the man took a key from her. The key had a bright yellow tag. I watched them go very thoughtfully.

"You can leave a message for her," said the hat, keeping up butteriness with difficulty whilst the new tenants were still in earshot. "I'll see she gets it, *if* she comes back."

I said there was no message. Eyeing me sourly, as if she had decided I was the cause of many a young girl's downfall, she said, "Well, if you don't need anything. This is my night off."

I followed her slowly downstairs and walked round the corner out of sight of the house. There I took out my key-ring, now also carrying the Yale from Laurel's handbag. It had a bright yellow tag "No. 25". And Lorna's address was 25, Gateside Circle!

I wanted to feel elated, but my mind jogged me solemnly about "Victor" Barnes. That's what you got for jumping to conclusions. It looked like a similar key to the one I had seen handed to the newlyweds, but perhaps half the flats in London had a fashion in these keys just now.

Even with a key, I drew the line at house-breaking.

What in heaven's name did I hope to find in a strange woman's flat, anyway? There was this unexplained coldness creeping over me again – why should Laurel have Lorna's key in her bag? Especially as Lorna had been away

98

from the flat for some time and, according to Laurel, she had not visited Gateside Circle before as Lorna had taken the flat just before we met.

A hideous idea I had toyed with for some time, became a sickening conviction . . .

Lorna had lent Laurel the flat for her assignations with "Vic"!

CHAPTER NINE

From the expresso bar across the road, I saw the beehive hat board a bus into town. Nonchalantly, I wandered across the road, and up the stairs. The corridor outside Lorna's flat was deserted. Whilst I fumbled with the key, from behind closed doors came muted homely sounds – the telly, a child crying, someone singing.

Taking a deep breath, I cautiously opened the door.

What if Lorna were sitting there? Waiting . . .

The living-room was quite empty. It was reassuringly tidy too.

The sinister scene behind the locked door – the strange man lying dead on the floor (who later turned out to be Vic) – were blessedly only imagination, the result of too many movies, with too many corpses on deserted apartment floors.

And yet – although there was nothing tangible, this sinister feeling of implied violence remained.

I stepped over a sea of papers and letters (the latter all depressingly alike in manilla envelopes, suggested bills) Small wonder she hadn't left a forwarding address! In the tiny kitchen, the refrigerator was empty, the electricity switched off. It looked as if (with the notable exception of a forwarding address), her journey had been well planned, for the cupboards except for a few tins and tired looking packets of cereal, were empty too.

Concluding that it was the forlorn, desperately orderly, look of an unoccupied hotel bedroom that worried me, I went into the bedroom. There was a lot of dust everywhere and feeling like someone who had strayed into the wrong TV play (a private eye in everything but courage), I opened one or two drawers in a desultory sort of way. As they were all practically empty, I opened the wardrobe.

It was packed full. Its rails choked with coats, suits, dresses, sweaters!

Either Lorna had a film-star's wardrobe, or had gone abroad, relying on some fine un-British weather, for she hadn't taken one of the four luxurious and almost new raincoats hanging there.

A funny thing – all her shoes were missing! Except for a pair of shapeless rather large mules, hastily kicked off and half hidden by the bed. Ah well, perhaps she had trouble with her feet, poor thing!

That wardrobe was a puzzle. Had she found a rich man who had promised her the earth? Or was he just highly sensitive about colour? For although some of the clothes looked new and felt expensive, she didn't have two things that went together. Just a fearful hotch-potch of agonising colours, specialising in purples and reds.

Poor girl, I had never realised that colour-blindness, a modest enough affliction in a man, must have been absolute hell for a woman.

As I stood there wondering what to do next, the disquieting sense of loss continued. Probably because it was so quiet. Soon it would be dark.

I hardly heard the light step in the hall until the tap of high heels was right outside the door.

Paralysed I waited, wondering what on earth James Bond would have done in these humiliating circumstances. I never found out for my luck held and the footsteps pattered on.

Now feeling weak and scared, as well as guilty, I decided to be a sheep at housebreaking instead of a lamb, and firmly drawing the curtains, switched on the light and examined the dressing-table's contents again in a business-like fashion.

There were odd nylons twisted together, some tired looking underwear, shabby gloves and scarves – just the usual weary garments any girl would abandon before she went on holiday.

The tiny bathroom was surprising though. Besides dusty bottles of expensive make-up and perfume, there was even a toothbrush and sponge bag. I shook my head – it was tantamount to a man departing without his shaving equipment.

Well, if I expected evidence of Vic, I was bitterly disappointed, having found precisely nothing and, for my pains, I was left with the guilty unclean feeling that I would never make a professional snooper.

Going back into the living-room, I solved that bleak forlorn look. Pictures, ornaments, bric-a-brac give something of their owner's personality too. There were none. Or perhaps Lorna had removed them everything but a revolting "doggie" calendar, a fat spaniel with a face uncommonly like Eva's.

Hardly blaming her for abandoning it, and steeling myself to avoid its wistfully familiar brown eyes, I noticed that the days had been scored out neatly – up to August. Propping it up again, it slithered down from the mantel-piece and landed in the hearth.

Then, I saw that in the empty fireplace, a batch of papers had been burnt. They lay in heavy charcoaled layers – not newspapers, surely! Something much heavier to give that solid blistered look. Photographs or books, shiny-surfaced.

It all fitted the theory of a new man.

Well, good luck to them! It looked as if Lorna had got a man after her own heart at last, providing new clothes and trips abroad, one that she loved sufficiently to destroy all pictures of the past. Idly stirring the ashes with my foot,

I wondered sadly if there had been pictures of "Lorna and Laurel" from their brief singing partnership.

By the window stood a small cheap writing desk. It, too, was empty. Closing the drawer below with difficulty, there was a rasping sound at the back and taking out the drawer, a folded brown foolscap envelope was wedged between the upper portion of the desk and the lower.

In it were a few pathetically lukewarm press cuttings of Lorna Blagdon in her various roles, and two small photographs stamped "proof". Sepia head and shoulder photos of two girls – profile and full face.

One of the girls was Laurel.

The terrible feeling of being with the dead grew stronger, of being haunted by a girl staring over my shoulder wearing a headscarf, a girl with Laurel's face, whispering.

Completely unnerved, I fled downstairs, took the wrong turning in the dusk and a man who was standing in the shadows of the front door just about shed his skin, when I cannoned right into him.

I was on the bus half-way into town when I remembered where I had seen him before. Not then looking startled or unguarded, just uncommunicative, he had been sitting in the bus reading a newspaper, the morning I went to Sycamore Grove in search of "Victor" Barnes!

CHAPTER TEN

The Rowe's Vale train was almost empty. I had eaten nothing since lunch, so I retired to put up my feet in solitary splendour, armed with some anaemic-looking meat sandwiches and a cup of scalding hot station tea. As I ate, I considered.

With a lugubrious lurch, aided by whistles, flags and asthmatic protest, the train moved feebly out of the station. Considering the number of passengers, I didn't much fancy the chances of this branch line's survival with its steam-train of a bygone age.

After a couple of miles of suburbia, we slammed hard into the dark bowels of the earth and acrid smoke poured into the open window. Suddenly I heard a yell in the corridor and a man, his body half-hidden by the enveloping smoke, struggled to close an open door. "I can't get it shut!" he yelled at me frantically.

"Hold on! I'll give you a hand." Both engulfed in the peculiar sulphuric hell of railway tunnels, we put our hands on the door which was now practically in free orbit. The taller of the two, I summoned my extra inches to lean forward and grasp the leather thong.

Then, to my surprise and horror, the man's hands instead of helping with the business of securing the door, were busy in the small of my back – pushing, thrusting me out into the stream of air.

The lights of the tunnel swam past as I clung giddily, one foot dangling into thin air. I couldn't hold much longer, the pressure was unbearable. Something cracked down on my shoulder – my hands were slipping, slipping . . . The roar of the wheels grew louder, nearer –

There was a voice. A voice of sanity and authority. "Here, what's going on there?" it demanded. "Come away from that door!"

The would-be assassin made a great show of dragging me back into the corridor. As the porter angrily and slickly caught the door and closed it, and the smoke subsided, I had a glimpse of a small putty-faced man with thinning hair.

He said indignantly, "We nearly had an accident, you know, trying to close that damned door. Mustn't have been properly locked before we left the station." He looked at me, his narrow eyes holding just a gleam of disappointment. "This chap was nearly a gonner."

Dazed and giddy, rubbing my shoulder where something hard, like the man's briefcase, had been used as a battering ram, suddenly the corridor was full of the people who seem to spend all their lives in gruesome expectation of fatal accidents.

"That man!" I gasped, "That man – he tried to push me out."

"Come along, sir," said the porter, "he was just trying to help. No need to upset yourself!"

"I tell you he tried to kill me," I looked round. "Where is he? Don't just stand there – he's getting away."

He was disappearing along the corridor, along with the other disappointed passengers. There was nothing now but the evil smell of sulphur and a few wisps of smoke, as we whipped out of darkness into the open country again.

The porter was persuading me back into my compartment. "You just have a quiet seat, sir. Try and take things easy – you've had a nasty shock, no doubt about it. I'll see if I can get you a cup of tea."

It was pointless to argue, so waiting until he was out of

sight, I searched the length and breadth of that train for the man who had just tried to kill me.

A couple of stations before Rowe's Vale, my vigilance was rewarded. I was sure it was the same man, now wearing a cap, scurrying through the barrier, with his raincoat collar well up.

It was curious that I hadn't recognised him – I'd know him next time. The same man who had followed me to Sycamore Grove, who had waited patiently outside Lorna's flat and then tried to push me off the train.

If it hadn't been for the train incident, I would have thought Inspector Wiggs was being over-conscientious. But shoving someone you despised back under their stone, in a metaphorical way, was far from shoving them into eternity, via a very messy kind of death.

The attempt fairly smacked of Hartley Rowe, at his ingenuous best.

In a grim kind of way it was heartening to prove beyond doubt, in my mind, that I was on to something Rowe didn't want known.

The near accident shed illumination on another thing. How very easy it was to contrive a fall from a train. Had Lady Marsden-Smith's death indeed been an accident? Or had she received a helping push from a man pretending to be a porter?

If a man three-quarters my size and weight had almost succeeded, what chance would Lady Celia have had against a man of the dimensions to fill the porter's suit? What was to have stopped him lying low and getting off the train a couple of stops before Rowe's Vale either?

The brown envelope containing the photos of Laurel and Lorna was suddenly a bolt of lightning and just like a snap of the fingers, I had it!

No wonder Rowe was anxious to get rid of me. If what

I thought I had unearthed was right, it was – to quote Callum – "no for bairns tae play wi'!"

As if thinking of Callum had the effect of conjuring up the devil, in the flat, having a ball, were three jolly farmers.

Tom, the old dinosaur himself, was cracking his ancient saurian hide at Callum's raw jokes about bulls and cows. Sandy Mac, that young-old man whose disproportionately long arms and legs gave him a look of not having evolved with the same speed as the rest of Homo sapiens sat at the table happily cradling my whisky bottle. His face, under the peaked bonnet, looking more like a well-skelped backside than ever. He was lustily bawling "Mhairi's Wedding."

"Aye, we got here this forenoon," said Callum, gravely shaking my hand. "We went along to yon Rowe's and a lassie, Miss Black," his eyes sparkled, "told us ye werna' there, but let us have a wee look at the painting. Man, thon's a bonny job, a bonny job," he said beaming proudly and slapping my raw aching shoulder. "Then Mr. Rowe – a nice-like wee feller – why, he took us into his office and the lassie made us coffee and we all had a bra' wee chat!"

"Man, he couldna' do enough for us, when he heard I was your brother. Told us all about your fine work, sounded that pleased. Och aye!"

(Och aye! I thought firmly and freely translated as "I'll bet!") I could just see Callum and Hartley Rowe clacking away like a couple of hens on a battery. Then Callum confirmed my worst fears. Looking concerned, he said, "Mr. Rowe tells me ye've no been awfa' weel lately – och!" Again the heavy hand descended and I fully expected to see my raw shoulder come away in his hand. "Och, laddie, ye'll be fine when we get ye home again. Just working too hard! Mr. Rowe said it himself, a fine conscientious laddie, he called ye! We're a' tae have lunch wi' him tomorrow afore we board the train." He

107

shook his great leonine head approvingly. "Aye, a real homely body, money or no'."

"I'm not going," I said shortly.

Callum's black brows rose like the spans of the Forth Bridge. "No' going!" he said in shocked angry tones. "Why ever no'? It's sich a treat."

"Mhairi's Wedding" had stopped. "Tch-tch" had taken its place as Sandy Mac echoed, "Sich a treat-like!"

I saw two couthy farmers, their lunch with the famous Rowe's the talking point of their holiday. What if I said Rowe had tried to murder me? If Callum had roared at his "wee brither" being married, he'd have to be carried away at this!

"You can go yourselves," I said grudgingly. "If you want to."

They wanted to.

After a night's sleep mercilessly abbreviated by the three jolly farmers happy on five hours, (I felt subhuman on less than eight) Callum stood before the mirror, manoeuvring his large red neck into a tight white collar.

Meeting my sombre reflection, I decided that Callum, after sleeping in a chair most of the night, and nearly fifteen years my senior, still looked a vastly healthier prospect than I did. He caught me watching him and asked idly, "Do ye no fancy that lassie?"

"Which lassie?" I asked dully, knowing perfectly well who he meant. "Eva," he said.

"Oh! Not really!"

Callum shook his great head. "Aye, she'd make a fine wife for some mannie." When I didn't answer, he continued, not unkindly, "Ye're nearly thirty, Gregor Roy, time ye was settling down, raising some bairns."

I wanted to yell, to shake him, to din forcibly into his thick skull that I *was* married – and separated – and widowered – instead I said, "True. But Eva's not for me."

Carefully he adjusted his tie, and brushed back the heavy black hair, still untouched by grey. A fine figure of a man was Callum. How he'd managed to steer clear of marriage all these years intrigued me (and all the unmarried girls in the Glen!) There was talk of some girl who had let him down long ago, but Callum could teach clams their business when he liked.

I said pointedly, "Eva would make a grand farmer's wife. Loves animals and small helpless creatures. Strong as a horse too!"

"Aye, I was thinking the verra same thing," said Callum, fairly dousing himself in the after-shave lotion that Eva had brought me from Madrid. Perhaps they used it there to repel the bulls. It certainly repelled me!

In the living-room, Sandy Mac was on a conducted tour of Tom's treasures, examining them with his eyes out on stalks and asking, "Is tha' a fac'?" between whiles "heel-for-heel and toe-for-toeing" it at Mhairi's Wedding.

The telephone rang. It was Hartley Rowe. He didn't sound dashed when I answered, merely hoped that I would come to their luncheon with my brother and his friend. That we could bury the past and part as friends. Perhaps I could help Mrs. Rowe plan her new colour scheme for the lounge – it would kill two birds with one stone. I said I wasn't sure whether I could make it, none too happy with his ominous choice of proverbs.

Why should Hartley Rowe specially want me, far less Mrs. Rowe who didn't apparently share her husband's talents as an actor? Why all the guff about parting as friends?

Looking at Callum and Sandy chatting with Tom, who had taken on a new lease of life since they came, everything seemed so normal. Maybe I *was* crazy, obsessed with nightmarish dreams of smiling villains.

Yet, the magnanimity of Hartley Rowe was just a thought too eager. What good, charitable reason could

109

he have for inviting two raw rough Scots farmers to a polite little luncheon? They weren't for sale. They were of no use to him in his devious world – except *as a lever to use against me*! Well, I'd go – just to thwart him. After all, he didn't know for certain how much I knew, and nothing could happen in a roomful of people, anyway.

Which just goes to show how wrong you can be.

Going to that little luncheon was practically the greatest mistake I had ever made.

CHAPTER ELEVEN

Leaving Callum and Sandy Mac in Eva's care, on the morning of Hartley Rowe's lunch, I went to Weschester Station. I had been right about Callum smacking his lips over Little Eva. However, it came as a shock to realise that she actually enjoyed his heavy humour, and went into paroxysms over his earthy jokes. This was certainly a new Miss Black!

At the station, the head porter gave me a very odd look. "Yes, a jacket and cap did go missing from the porter's room a while back," and looking at the number on the cap, he frowned, "This looks like it, right enough. Half-a-jiff and I'll get Bob for you." He tapped the garments with his knuckles. "He'll be amazed to see these. There was a lot of trouble about them at the time. Found them, you did say?" he asked cautiously, and seeming reluctant to let me out of his sight, he shouted to another porter, "Find Bob, will you? Tell him it's urgent."

Excusing himself, he withdrew to an inner sanctum, where I heard the click and ring of a telephone and some undecipherable but highly confidential whispering.

Returning, he looked very pleased and took an extraordinary time and a lot of pencil sharpening to get down my name and address, plus an ingenuous amount of irrelevant details.

By the time we were both desperately wondering how much longer he could possibly spin it out – his anxious neck-cranings towards the long empty platform wouldn't have deceived a blind kitten – a Mr. Wilson bustled in, out of breath and trying to make the visit look coincidental, he described himself as a railway detective.

To say they looked disbelieving when I repeated the history of the jacket and cap, in my suitcase, in Left Luggage, is a mammoth understatement.

Wilson asked abruptly: "When did you leave it?" watching the garments in question sternly, as if they were stubbornly refusing to reveal all.

"The suitcase had been on loan to a friend," I said.

"Could we have this person's name and address?" asked Wilson, a shade impatiently.

This was getting more involved than I liked, and when I said, "Laurel Marsden-Smith," there was an audible gasp from the head porter. Wilson, more used to controlling his feelings, asked quietly: "The same Miss Marsden-Smith who er – died recently?"

I said yes and produced the remains of the label which had once adhered to the side of the case. "The number's still legible – you should be able to trace the ticket from Left Luggage. The date was 21st October – you know, the day Lady Marsden-Smith fell out of the train."

A sharp look from Wilson suggested that I was teaching my grandmother how to suck eggs. "Is it now? You seem to know a lot about it," he said heavily, having decided this was a Johnny Know-all, whom he would enjoy pulling down to size. "May I ask where you were when all this happened, Mr. MacGregor?"

"In Edinburgh." I scribbled on a piece of paper, "Here's the hotel and my room number." Mr. Wilson looked a very disappointed man.

The porter Bob arrived, angry and defensive. He was the picture of a man who had made many appearances before his boss, and always found himself in a heap of trouble. Reluctantly, he confirmed the garments as his. "I told you I'd lost them," he said triumphantly to the head porter. "Who'd want these old togs, anyway?

What was it? Kids having a joke?" Bob was, as I had suspected, a big solid toughly built man.

"When did you lose them?" asked Wilson.

Bob groaned. "Oh, not again. Look, I gave you all the details at the time. I can't remember exactly – Blackberry week – October sometime. There were other things, too, remember?" he said darkly to the head porter and scratching his bald head, continued with a sense of grievance. "Some blighter reported that I had been insolent and put him off at the wrong station – I'd never been on the perishing train in the first place. I was right here on duty, even if it was my number he reported. Lucky I could prove it too." and looking angrily at Wilson, "Though some people seemed sorry to believe what they'd seen with their own eyes."

"We don't need to trouble Mr. MacGregor with all this," said Wilson stiffly, and apparently running out of further questions, and seeing that Bob was likely to damage someone's prestige if he stayed around long enough, they reluctantly let me go.

When I looked back, all three were watching from the door of the office, as if they thought I might sprout horns and a tail. They stared, puzzled and doubtful, as if by watching long enough, they'd get me red-handed, lifting something bigger – like a train – next time.

On the bus out to Hartley Rowe's, I felt very pleased with myself. I was hungry, and looking forward to lunch and a battle of wits with mine host. I'd have to humour Callum about some reason for staying here a bit longer. I was pretty certain now that Lady Celia had been murdered, and there were other things to prove. One in particular, a diabolical suspicion, I hardly dared contemplate.

The Rowe house situated in the Dales three miles beyond Vansett Bridge, must have cost a cool two hundred thousand, and my feet ached by the time I had negotiated the mile-long drive. On the outside, there was everything, including a miniature Kew garden and a heated swimming-pool.

The inside was in keeping with the grand approaches and Hartley Rowe didn't let me down once by expensive vulgarity. The pictures on the walls alone, were worth a fortune. I fairly goggled at famous artists. Even the reproductions of the pictures would have been beyond me, but here were the originals themselves, genuine hand-painted autographed masters!

I thought of my ghastly mural and groaned. Great art humbles me now. Long ago, I was daft enough to feel inspired, but that was before plumbing the depths of my limited talents. The kindest verdict anyone could give was "competent". The fire of greatness had passed by. It would never come now.

Hartley Rowe's inspiration and hard cash showed in his collection of antiques too. A shrewd and tasteful buyer, he must have had someone permanently stationed at all the world's great auctions. The furniture was magnificent and I got my only laugh that day at the sight of Callum and Sandy Mac, perched uncomfortably on Louis Quatorze chairs, solemnly regarding each other's muckle great feet, ludicrously nestling on the fabulous Aubusson carpet.

Mrs. Rowe was being delectable, so affable that I was already having trouble remembering her as Frosty Voice. As hospitable as she was charming, my sherry glass was never empty.

All the while, she talked of her decorating problems, with the same intensity that other people talk about their in-laws or the children's education, and tenderly escorted me round that superb museum of a house.

No other guests were apparent. Perhaps we had mistaken the time? Certainly, in that period before anyone else arrived, I mellowed considerably. I suggested colours, materials, décors for the lounge and felt that I had grossly misjudged Mrs. Rowe, who gave little girlish screams of delight and clasped her hands ingenuously at my suggestions.

My natural chivalry (plus a large quantity of sherry) suggested that behind that enamelled mask there was a heart of gold. Poor dear soul, a loyal and true wife! Touching the envelope in my pocket, I wept for the day when she must learn, alas, she was married to a fiend – an unmitigated villain, who would not even stop at murder.

Hartley Rowe's sentimental wringing of my hand, whilst he watched, cool and detached, from behind that sad clown's face, did nothing to quell my suspicions. And all the time, at my elbow, like the widow's cruse, was a sherry glass that mysteriously refilled itself . . .

When lunch was announced, I was glowing, prepared to compliment everyone and everything. I was just sober enough to recognise the rose-bedecked hat anew and under it the lady to whom Mrs. Rowe had talked of Vic, at the mural's unveiling.

Mrs. Rowe was busy elsewhere and during her relaxed vigilance, I leaned over and said to the friend with the roses, "Lovely day!"

She smiled vaguely, wondering who on earth I could be. "Remember we met the other day?" I said.

"Oh, yes of course," she held out her hand, "How are you?" without the slightest clue to my identity.

"Tell me, is Vic coming today?" I asked, "Wanted a word with him."

She giggled. "Well, look – he's over there. Right behind you, talking to Judith Rowe."

I turned my head slowly. There was only one person with Mrs. Rowe. A man whose great bulk was easily recognisable as Dr. Gerald Fellton. They were talking very seriously, heads down – and make no mistake, they were talking about me.

The unknown said, in tones of friendly affection. "They're not a bit alike, are they?"

"Alike? Should they be alike?" I asked.

"Well – you'd never take them for brother and sister, would you." She thought for a moment. "Apart from their eyes. Don't you think they've got the same eyes?"

I did indeed. I remembered wondering that day in the surgery where I had seen pale eyes like Gerald Fellton's before.

Were they all in it? A nice little murderous family set-up, with Fellton's sister married to Hartley Rowe, who was Lady Marsden-Smith's third – or was it fourth – cousin?

"Are you a patient of Vic's?" The lady was obviously keen for gossip. "I can't imagine when he does his doctoring, mind you. Always on the golf course. They say he has quite an eye for the women, too. Of course, what can you expect, he must be getting on." As she talked she eyed Fellton, glass in hand, looking distinctly regretful, perhaps at his amorous possibilities.

"Oh, excuse me." I saw Eva coming and sprang to my feet. Only I didn't spring, I lurched, wobbled and practically fell. Something had happened to my legs. Making a grab at Eva's arm, my coordination wasn't too good either. Gulping down the rest of the sherry, I concluded that I'd like a look at the label on that bottle. It was powerful stuff.

"Oh, hello," said Eva, markedly unenthusiastic.

"What's that you're drinking?"

"A very large whisky – but it happens to be for Callum," she said, with a giggle.

"Hold on! What's the L in Gerald L. Fellton?"

She eyed me coldly. "Very funny! Is this a new game?"

"No. Er – Callum was asking me," I lied brazenly.

She melted visibly. "Lancelot – no! One of those odd

116

names – you know, stagey! I remember – Ludovic! Yes, Ludovic."

"Off you go with the whisky, dear," I purred, as Mrs. Rowe agitatedly sought me, burdened down with a full decanter of sherry.

I can't recall what was on the menu, but long before we reached the sweet, some very curious looks were coming my way, from necks craned politely up and down the table.

Something weird had happened to my spine, and try as I might, even the old trick of measuring my back against the bony Sheraton dining chair, face down I went again, like a child's wobbly man.

I must have fresh air.

Then, around the middle of the rich carpet, the pile on it began to grow – knee-high, waist-high – when it was shoulder-high, I started swimming and drowned in its suffocating folds.

CHAPTER TWELVE

I awoke to the pleasant sensation of being rocked gently, and discovered that I was lying full-length in the back of someone's car. The soft cushion turned out to be Eva's ample lap.

She looked down accusingly. "You passed out, Greg. My, what a fool *you* made of yourself. Why on earth did you drink so much?" She sounded angry and reproachful, and I sat up with a suddenness that shook a myriad of stars dancing in my head.

"I've never passed out through drinking in my life," I said thickly, but virtuously indignant.

"Well, you can count to-day as the first time," she said. "It was obvious, even before the lunch began, that you'd had a bucket. I don't know! Really I don't." She threw this helpless remark to someone who sat opposite.

I turned my head painfully to observe Callum and Sandy Mac looking black-affronted – two kids deprived of their candy and embarked on a big sulk.

"What did I do that was so terrible, anyway? Did I punch anybody's nose?" I asked hopefully.

"You tried to swim across the carpet. Mr. Rowe and Dr. Fellton got you into the morning room and there you lay snoring until we had finished lunch. Then Mr. Rowe gave us his car to take you to the station. I'm just here to see you off safely," said Eva, with a coy and flirtatious glance over at Callum.

"Steady on," I said, "I'm staying here – I'm not going anywhere."

"Ye're coming home wi' us, laddie – before you get into more mischief," said Callum grimly.

I tried to sit up, to give weight to my dignified protest at being hi-jacked. The effort was agonising and as the car chose that moment to swing round into the station yard, jelly-like and unresistant I landed back in Eva' s lap.

"I hadna' any idea how bad the laddie was," said Callum with a sad shake of his great head. "Poor Mr. Rowe – makin' sich a fool o' the wee mannie. What awfu' things to say! Aye, d'ye ken, Eva?" (Eva, was it? My head noted wearily).

"Fancy saying someone tried to push you off a train," said Eva with just the suspicion of a giggle.

"Come on, Sandy man, gie us a hand." And protesting vigorously supported firmly by Callum and Sandy Mac, with Eva bringing up the rear, I teetered into the station. By this time I was heartily sick of people trying to push me on or off trains without my consent and I determined that this time there would be a fight.

If only they'd stop racing pell-mell down the platform! If only they'd let me get my breath! Oh, God, I feel so weary!

I yawned. A minute or two to gather my strength and make a run for it . . .

I had hardly closed my eyes when the train's jolting stirred me to irritated consciousness. Opening one eye revealed a small disaster. Eva had gone. I lay sprawled along one side of the compartment. Opposite, Callum and Sandy Mac played Pontoon, occasionally refreshing themselves from the small crate of beer cans at their feet. Trees and telegraph poles belted past the windows at a hideous speed.

Furiously I sat up, immediately regretting it, when the top of my head kept on going up.

"Here, give me some of that! God, I feel awful!" I made a grab at a beer can, missed it completely and was

119

further humiliated by Callum patiently handing one over with great dignity.

"Aye, ye've recovered, I see. And a pretty dance ye've led everybody, my braw laddie."

"I haven't started yet! If you want to see some pretty dances being led, you just wait until I get my hands on Hartley Rowe again."

"That'll do now! That'll do!" warned Callum, shaking his head and glowering from under his heavy black hair. "I dinna ken what's got in ye, laddie. Getting tae big fer yer breeks, is that the way o' it? Winnin' a' they grand prizes has gone tae yer wee head, right enough!" he taunted. "And what about this poor lassie ye're insisting is wed tae ye – asking poor Mr. Rowe about her – and her deid and gone."

The shake of his head and the glowering expression were tantalisingly familiar. I wondered why, until the fleeting sight of Black Aberdeen Angus cattle grazing in a field jogged my memory. A great bull of a man was brother Callum – a great, stubborn, Aberdeen Angus bull of a man!

And Sandy Mac at his side, with his long sad chinless red face, chewing gum was like the blood brother to a farmyard goat. God knows if people really begin to resemble the animals they associate with, but it made a sobering thought.

Callum sat back, thumping both fists on to navy serge-clad thighs which looked as if they might split open in revenge. "It's no like ye, Gregor Roy – no like ye at a'," he said, appealing to my better self, alas long departed! "Ye were always that gentle as a wee laddie, always helpful and heedful to ither folks views. Ye've shamed me right enough, me that's been father and mother tae ye for fifteen year – " (and hadn't he reminded me of that almost daily for the past fourteen?) "Many's a one would hae ye working on the croft, but I let ye hae

120

yer head. And now, where's all those fancy notions got ye?"

Sandy Mac stopped chewing long enough to observe, as if I were absent and merely the subject of a private conversation between them "Aye, it's a' that daft education ye gie'd him, Callum Iain – ye mark my words, I always said nae guid wad come o' it. A' them daft-like colleges, filling folks heids wi' a lot o' nonsense."

Ignoring Sandy Mac, I said, "Listen to me, Callum! I really was married to this girl Laurel." Patiently I tried to explain it once more, but about quarter-way through the story (and not a tenth-way through to Callum) I gave up.

It sounded so corny. A bit of homely rape, incest or seduction, a shot-gun wedding, Callum could have understood and relished. These were the events that formed the backbone of most of our Scots history anyway but not this fairy tale of an heiress marrying a penniless artist for a whim.

"Whoever heard of sich-like goings-on?" he appealed to Sandy Mac with a shake of his great head.

"Oh, shut up!" I said angrily. How could I expect a simple honest dealing man like my brother to understand the tortuous machinations behind the scenes at Rowe's?

I moved my head but the nuts and bolts were still in free orbit. God knows what Mrs. Rowe, aided and abetted by Fellton, and her husband, had put in the sherry – some kind of truth drug by the sound of it. I'd have kicked myself if I'd had strength, for apparently I had been nicely obliging and given the show away.

Now that Rowe knew, or guessed, one thing was clear. Time was running out. I had to get right back and bend Inspector Wiggs' unbelieving ear. I could hear his long-suffering sigh.

But first, getting off this train was going to need some remarkable strategy.

Feeling in my pocket, I had a moment's panic. I searched again, and thankfully my hand encountered the envelope containing the photographs. I must have been looking in the wrong pocket.

"You might have given me time to say goodbye to Eva and Tom," I said, expressing sentiments that Callum would appreciate. "And what about the rest of my things?"

"You werena' in a state to say goodbye to anyone," said Callum glumly.

"An' that's a fac'," echoed Sandy Mac.

"Just rolled into the train, lay down and asleep like a bairn afore we pulled out." Callum gave me a puzzled look. "Never thocht a brother o' mine – a direct descendant o' Rob Roy MacGregor, too – would hae sich a poor-like stomach for the drink. Ye maun be getting soft, Gregor Roy – when ye was a student, ye could knock the drappies back nae bother. I never kenned ye fu' at a'."

I hardly liked to remind him that the drappies under discussion had not been drugged. I had to thank the steady consumption of whisky during the last couple of weeks which had immunised my system to the drug's stronger effects. Otherwise I would have lain comatose long after we crossed over the Forth Bridge, which was precisely what Hartley Rowe had intended.

"We packed the rest o' yer things at the flat, and Eva kindly suggested sending anything else on. Ye can always write to Tom – and Eva. Anyway," he coughed and frowned severely at the telegraph posts whizzing past the window, "anyway, it's like enough ye'll be seeing Eva again – at Christmas."

"It's like that, is it?" I said.

He turned and grinned. "Like that, Gregor Roy! I canna bear waste, whether it be beast or man, fodder or fuel. And you lassie's just wasting her best years, when by the look and strength o' her, she'd do grand on the croft – aye, in the bed, too, doubtless."

"She'll want marriage, Callum," I said, purposely mis-understanding.

"Marriage, is it?" he shouted, banging his great hams of fists together. "And I'll hae ye ken, it's marriage that I'm intending."

"No kidding," I said drily, and standing up carefully, removed my sheepskin jacket from the rack. As I struggled into it, both men were immediately on their feet like punchy boxers in the ring.

"And where d'ye think ye're going?" demanded Callum.

"Nowhere. I'm cold, that's all." I sat down with a picture paper they had cast aside, engrossing myself in the latest extra-matrimonial exploits of a pneumatically-bosomed film star. Slyly, I watched Callum and Sandy Mac exchange looks of relief and fall to their cards again.

The peaceful journey over the next few miles was broken only by Sandy Mac's damnable whistling, and Callum's volcanic sighs as his gambling losses reached the unprecedented heights of twenty-four pence.

They fairly punished that crate of beer too, until first Callum, then immediately he returned, Sandy Mac, disappeared down the corridor.

Swiftly we sped through the last station before York.

I folded the paper. The time had come.

CHAPTER THIRTEEN

I stood up, stretching and yawning, and immediately my two jailers went into their Jacks-in-the-Box routine.

"Oh, sit down, for God's sake," I snapped wearily, "I'm just going along the corridor."

"What for?" demanded Callum.

"The same as you've been for," I said angrily. "I'm not a camel, either. Relax! What's worrying you? I can't go anywhere. You presumably have the tickets?"

Leaving them looking at each other dubiously, I hurried down the corridor. As I hoped, the first toilet was engaged and as fast as light I put the entire length of the train between us. By the time I reached the guard's van, the train was slowing down, preparing to negotiate the approaches to the vast arterial junctions that foreshadow York Station.

I looked out. The signalbox was on the other side of the train, so choosing a moment when the train was doing all of five miles per hour, I jumped, and landed on solid ground between a lot of rails.

It was going to take a little time to work swiftly across the lines, which criss-crossed and interweaved in a dizzying fashion, particularly since the effects of fresh air, a cold night and a playful breeze had made the top of my head unscrew in an unpleasantly skittish manner. At the moment, I needed luck, all my senses and a few extra pairs of eyes throw in. I didn't particularly fancy a train in the backside, and the man in the signal box needed watching too, or I'd land in jail. Luckily, it was too dark for the men with their little croquet mallets to be playing games on the lines.

Who said something about luck? Suddenly the air was split by a furious yell and the sound of heavy footsteps. I took to my heels and sprinted over those last few yards, cursing and praying, all at the same time.

Hauling myself breathlessly on to a platform, thankful that my arms and legs were still intact, I loped over a wooden fence and dropped down on to a narrow deserted road, which seemed to run alongside a goods yard.

I crouched down, listening. Everything was silent. My pursuers had apparently given up the chase, and ten minutes later I was riding through York on a southbound bus which brought Rowe's Vale some twenty miles nearer.

After thumbing a couple of lifts, I reached the Rowe Arms at midnight. They didn't know me from Adam, and as I was unaccompanied, didn't seem particularly interested in my lack of luggage.

In the bedroom, which offered monastic comfort, but at least was centrally heated, I picked up the telephone. It was too late to talk to Tom, who had enough troubles to keep him awake half the night. Instead, I put in a call and left a message for Inspector Wiggs, then tumbled gratefully into bed.

I slept remarkably well, heavily and without dreams, probably still working off drugged sherries and the healthy exercise across the rails in York Station.

Someone brought early morning tea and I was asleep again immediately the empty cup clattered back on to its saucer.

Very much later, I surfaced to find a familiar figure munching his moustache, and Wiggs stood surveying the first bunting and flags being fixed in the square below. Presumably the Royal visit was one big headache for him, for he turned away from the window with a long, mournful sigh.

He grunted good-morning and surveyed my bare shoulders disapprovingly, as yet another slackening of the moral fibre of today's youth. Wrapping myself in a blanket, I said, "I don't usually sleep like this, I prefer striped winceyette any day. However, I hitch-hiked back from York last night, and hadn't time to get my luggage."

Wiggs eyed me doubtfully, and said stiffly that I might as well stay where I was most comfortable for our "little chat in private – except for the sergeant here."

Sitting in the only bedroom chair, feet together, nursing his helmet, was the quietest bobby I'd ever encountered. He had the kind of unblinking bright blue eyes, brown straight hair and great technicolour face commonly only seen on tailor's dummies. But by comparison, the waxworks figures in Madame Tussauds were a rowdy lot. Perhaps he had a clockwork breathing system too. He certainly managed it without a muscular quiver or solitary sound.

Wiggs remarked drily, "I called at your flat yesterday, but old Tom Markham said you'd gone off to Scotland unexpectedly with your brother." He paused and inquired politely, "Not bad news, I hope?" I said anything but, and he continued, "There are one or two questions I'd like to ask you. About the porter's suit which er – mysteriously appeared in your locked suitcase."

"Better get John Dickson Carr to explain that one," I said and out of the corner of my eye saw the sergeant's pencil suddenly poised above a notebook which had materialized like a conjurer's trick.

Wiggs shook his head irritably, presumably the sergeant lacked a clockwork sense of humour too. "This business about the missing jacket and cap has been nettling us for some time," he said. "Detective Wilson, whom you met," there was a poor thin ghost of a smile touching his mouth as he said, "consulted me privately about it."

"Really?" I said, watching the smile dissolve into

126

habitual bleakness as he asked me precisely the same questions as Wilson, and received precisely the same answers.

"Any ideas as to how the suit got into your suitcase?" he asked.

"Yes. I gave the case to my wife when we were in London. I had to go back to Scotland and can only presume she later put it in Left Luggage. At least, I found the spare key in her purse."

Biting his moustache frenziedly now, he asked, "And what might your wife's name and whereabouts be, please?"

"Laurel Marsden-Smith – deceased."

Poor Wiggs was human enough to almost burst a blood vessel at that. The bobby in the corner had obviously been impressed by the performance before, because he rapidly hitched his feet out of harm's way and shrank his large bulk well back into the chair. He looked, if possible, even less alive than ever.

"Now, look here," said Wiggs, "You're not trying to palm me off with that story again. I think it's only right to warn you, young fellow – "

"All right, all right! I'm sorry but it happens to be the truth. The reason I asked you to come, is that I think I can prove that I am speaking the truth. If at the end of it, you think I'm certifiable, well then – "

Wiggs gave a long-suffering sigh and sat down heavily on the bottom of the bed. "Come on, then, lets have it," he said sharply.

CHAPTER FOURTEEN

Feeling like an amateur conjurer sharing the top of the bill at the London Palladium with Paul Daniels, I said, "After Laurel's death, in her handbag, which was picked up after the accident, I found two keys." Stretching over to my jacket pocket, I took out the key ring. "This one, the spare for my suitcase – and a housekey, this Yale here." Wiggs examined them both silently. "There was also a Left Luggage ticket dated October 21st, which I duly exchanged for the suitcase, and this scrap of paper."

Wiggs read: "V.B.421!" and exclaimed "So what?"

"After my marriage to Laurel – "

Wiggs fairly danced with impatient rage, but managed to gulp out, "All right, all right – get on with it!"

"Thank you. After my marriage I went back to Scotland. The mural wasn't finished, but I still had to teach until they found someone else. Anyway, after I went away, Laurel got involved in a plot to murder her mother."

"Oh, for God's sake!" groaned Wiggs.

Pretending not to hear, I continued. "Her mother's fall from the train was carefully arranged in advance – probably assisted by a bogus porter in the stolen jacket and cap. After the "accident", he disappeared, leaving Laurel to raise the alarm just before they reached the next station. Unfortunately, in the interval, he fell foul of an irascible first-class gent, who reported his insolence, quoting his number, etc. If Wilson has discussed this with you, you'll realise that the real porter was seen on duty miles away."

Wiggs arranged his large feet heavily. "I suppose you can prove this incident was connected with Lady Marsden-Smith's death? There are a hundred other possibilities, most likely some crafty devil trying to travel without paying his fare."

"Well, if you decide to look for a murderer – he's a big man, something of the proportions of, say, Dr. Gerald Fellton."

"Why Dr. Fellton?" asked Wiggs sharply.

"Because his middle name is Ludovic, the Rowes call him Vic – and Laurel died saying his name."

Wiggs grunted. "It won't do, MacGregor. There's one big flaw. You could never convince anyone that Laurel Marsden-Smith deliberately contrived her mother's murder. They were absolutely inseparable. The girl made tremendous sacrifices for her." He paused and said slowly. "If you were really married to her, you surely know that. Didn't you claim her anxiety for her mother as the reason for all the secrecy?" He waited to let that sink in.

"For God's sake, MacGregor, when you can't even prove you were married to the girl, how can you expect anyone to swallow this fantastic story that she borrowed your suitcase? How can you prove the Left Luggage ticket was in her handbag, or what the case contained?" He weighed the small key in his hand. "It's no good, you know. This kind of luggage is sold in every big chain-store throughout the country. As you didn't have any identifying marks on it, it could be one of hundreds that are deposited in Left Luggage offices every day." He paused.

"You're making quite a case against *yourself*, don't you realise that? Trying to frame a dead girl with something that, if it was murder, could just as deviously be pinned on the person who really had something to gain by getting rid of her?"

"Who?"

"Well, for instance – you, MacGregor!"

129

"Why the devil should I want to kill her?"

He shrugged heavily. "You might be a crackpot – imagined she stood in your way with Laurel. Or you might be a fortune-hunter, feeling it was one step nearer laying your hands on some of the Rowe fortune."

"Very ingenious – except that I was in Edinburgh at the time – and can prove it."

"Well, alibis have been broken before now," he said laconically. "It's as likely a story – that you were in Edinburgh – as Laurel Marsden-Smith killing her own mother. You're surely not serious!"

"I am serious. The Laurel I knew and married, no, she would have been incapable of murder – but the Laurel you saw buried recently – she could have done it – and did."

"I don't follow you," said Wiggs drily.

I wasn't prepared to play my ace yet. "You will! Now, would you like to know how I got on to this train murder angle in the first place? You haven't got a man following me, by any chance?"

Wiggs snorted. "More to do with our time!"

"Well, this man who's been following me, tried to push me through an open carriage door in the train coming back to Rowe's Vale from London a couple of evenings ago."

Wiggs looked doleful. "You have evidence, witnesses, of course?"

"No I haven't. What sort of evidence do you want? My body lying on the line somewhere?"

"Well, what did he look like, this would-be murderer?" Wiggs asked sourly, sounding tired.

I described him and Wiggs looked even sadder. "I suppose you realise that your description fits half the male population of the British Isles."

"All right. Do you know how I came to spend the night here at the Rowe Arms, without as much as a toothbrush?"

Wiggs sigh was deep and sceptical.

130

"Hartley Rowe invited me to lunch yesterday, had his wife dope my sherry, then persuaded my brother and his friend to get me back to Scotland."

"Prove it!" said Wiggs quietly.

"Of course I can't prove it. There is one thing, though – "

"Ah, at last!" said Wiggs, with a blissful disbelieving smile. "How well did you know Laurel Marsden-Smith?"

Wiggs thought, then frowned. "Hardly at all, really. She's only been in England on very infrequent visits since she was a few years old and – " he stopped.

"And? Someone tried to kidnap her and scared the wits out of her mother," I said.

Wiggs was silent, his forefinger tracing the pattern on the edge of the quilt.

"Now don't you think the whole set-up's pregnant with possibilities for the criminally-inclined?"

"My dear boy," said Wiggs light-heartedly. "You read too many detective stories. I can assure you, it's the most innocent and natural thing amongst people whose only crime is having more money than original ways of spending it. So they live abroad most of the time, avoiding British winters or the tax-man, and sometimes both." He heaved back his shoulders. "And wouldn't we do the same with all that money?"

"All right. How would you describe Laurel Marsden-Smith?"

With the true policeman's eye for detail, he replied without hesitation. "About five feet tall, weighing slightly under eight stone, petite build, ash-blonde hair, blue eyes, aged twenty-one, but looked younger. Very attractive, elegantly dressed."

"Did you ever see her looking untidy or slovenly?"

"No, but I didn't see her often." He frowned looking puzzled. "She was always outstandingly well-dressed, clothes expensive – of course, she had the money to be both."

"What would you say if you saw her wearing a purple and cyclamen head-scarf, a tan coat, small bright red handbag and chocolate brown gloves."

Wiggs said impatiently, with a quick look at his watch. "I don't see what this fashion quiz has to do with it."

"I think you will!"

He sat back, assimilating the picture and gnawing at his moustache. "Probably got dressed in a terrible hurry," then he added slowly, with an indifferent shrug, humouring me, "Else maybe she was colour-blind." And he toppled neatly over into the net!

"Why?" I asked sharply.

He laughed uncomfortably. "Don't know, except that I'm colour-blind myself, and it's the sort of affliction where I can't tell reds and browns. A lot of chaps in the RAF were grounded by colour-blindness during the war."

That explained the ferocious handlebars. Once upon a time, twenty years ago, he had cherished dreams of being a pilot, now he was heavy, middle-aged and unglamorous.

"Are you saying that Laurel Marsden-Smith was colour-blind?" he said.

"No! But when I was in London, I thought I'd look up a friend of hers, Lorna Blagdon."

"The one she went on the stage with for a while?" asked Wiggs.

"The same! She wasn't at home, and while I was asking about her, one of the other tenants I noticed had an identical key to that one, you're holding – with the yellow tag." I paused. "Shall I tell you a significant thing about Lorna that I learned from Laurel?"

"She was colour-blind," said Wiggs sharply. "So you illegally entered her flat."

"Not so! The key was in my wife's handbag, remember? They were friends who had shared a flat at one time. Can

I finish or do I get the handcuffs now?" He ignored my outstretched wrists. "The girl's landlady said she hadn't been there for some time, so I went in. I thought there might be some letters, evidence in something Laurel had written, that would prove we were married."

I described the state of the flat, the emptiness all over, except for the wardrobe choked with clothes. Shoes gone, but in the bathroom toilet articles left behind. And in the fireplace all the burnt papers.

Slowly, savouring the moment, I drew out my ace. Handing him the brown envelope from Lorna's writing desk, I said, "This was jammed at the back of a drawer containing press-cuttings of Lorna Blagdon's career as an actress. There were also two photographs, of Laurel and Lorna, from their singing-sisters act."

Opening the envelope, he drew out the photos carefully. "You'll notice they're made up to look alike. Same hair-style, colour, etc. Now, doesn't an alarming possibility suggest itself? You know of course, how their singing act ended?"

Wiggs looked up. He seemed transfixed by the photos. "Something about a road accident. Dr. Fellton went over to Italy and brought Laurel home."

"That's interesting," I said, "Now supposing Fellton initially mistook Lorna, all bandaged about the face and arms, for Laurel. Supposing he then realised that with a bit of plastic surgery, which she would need anyway, he could make her Laurel's twin and dispose of Laurel. The Rowe fortune, which he and his brother-in-law had dreamed of possessing for years, would be theirs!"

Wiggs didn't say anything. He looked faintly glassy-eyed, his head well down into his collar.

"The set-up was perfect. A rich girl with no friends, tied to an invalid mother who was likely to die any moment with a rare heart disease, or be killed on the operating table by a dicey operation. Her recovery must

133

have thrown them into a fit of teeth-gnashing, unparalleled in the history of human misfortune. Then, they got the bright idea of pushing her off the train! However, to quote Robert Burns, "The best-laid schemes o' mice and men Gang aft a-gley". They didn't bargain for the real Laurel's secret love affair, and worse still her secret marriage."

Wiggs still didn't say a word. He just sat staring at the photographs. Exasperated, I pointed to them, "Surely you must see how easy it was to make the change-over. Laurel was maybe slightly smaller, with more delicate features and since all Lorna's shoes were missing, presumably Laurel had smaller feet. Lorna certainly had a bigger nose, but nothing outwith the bounds of plastic surgery. Fellton must know plenty of boys in the trade, although I'd bet it was done abroad, in all innocence that it was for a criminal cause."

And still there wasn't a cheep of triumph out of Wiggs. What was wrong with the man, was he made of wood? Then, very dolefully, he turned round and asked heavily, "Is this some sort of a game, MacGregor?"

"What do you mean?"

He laid the photographs face upwards on the bed. I blinked my eyes. Press-cuttings and pictures of Laurel and Lorna had gone. In their place were three pictures roughly the same size – of Rowe's new factory. I remembered that I had lain snoring in the morning-room in Rowe's house, that the envelope when I searched for it later, wasn't in the pocket where it should have been. I could have wept.

CHAPTER FIFTEEN

I tried to explain what had happened to Wiggs, but he just sighed and looked miserable. "I swear they were in there! You must believe me! Why the hell should I lie, anyway? I want my wife back! I want Laurel – I don't give a damn for the Rowe fortune, but believe me, while there's still time, for God's sake, help me to find her. Whoever did the switch over knows by now that I'm on to them, and Laurel's days will be numbered."

Wiggs and the bobby might have been bits of furniture in the hotel for all the notice they took of my appeal. I sat back wearily. What was the use? It was the same old nightmare I had lived with Laurel-Lorna, the trite words that no one wanted to hear or understand.

Very gingerly, and with obvious distaste, Wiggs scooped up the photographs of the factory and thrust them back into the envelope. He weighed it in his hand. "Perhaps it wasn't Laurel you married. Perhaps it was Lorna Blagdon. Have you thought of that?" He looked at me steadily for a moment, then stood up. "I think you'd better come along with us, young man."

"Am I being arrested?"

He shook his head. There was a curious look in his eyes, as if the vision of the flags outside the window was suddenly very satisfying. "We'll need to have an official statement, just to put you in the clear about the porter's jacket business. We'll wait for you downstairs."

Wiggs must have been doing a lot of constructive thinking in the interval in which it took me to get dressed, for

135

as we drove towards the police station, he said, "About that bogus porter idea. It couldn't have been Dr. Fellton. I seem to remember that he had an alibi – an emergency meeting in London, at the hospital, that day, or I expect he would have travelled back with Laurel and her mother on the train." He shrugged. "Well, that should be easy to check."

"Oh, I'm sure he's well ahead of you there. The body was found on the branch-line half-an-hour out of London. The train's first stop was at Wasley. What was to stop Fellton seeing her off alone, nipping into a toilet and changing into the porter? Laurel's mother could be guaranteed to recognise her own daughter, so some excuse had been made why Laurel couldn't come. Then using Lorna as a decoy, her semi-drugged mother was lured out into the corridor, with the train door ready open."

"The deed done, the porter's uniform was shoved into the unidentifiable suitcase. The train reached Wasley, Lorna raised the alarm and Fellton nipped out. With a fast car and good luck, he could have been back in London only slightly late for his meeting. Lorna couldn't abandon the suitcase on the train – too risky – but things can lie unclaimed in Left Luggage, until well after accident and stolen uniform were forgotten."

Wiggs said, "That note you found. V.B. something-or-other. Probably a 'phone number. They're all hundreds or thousands round here."

"You can save your money. I've tried that. It brought me a Mr. V. Barnes (first name Vincent), a laundry, a coal company and a hospital."

"That's it!" said Wiggs triumphantly. "V.B.421! The Rowe Vale Private Clinic. Vansett Bridge 421. No wonder it was so familiar!"

In a suspiciously cell-like room, which made the monastic furnishings of the Rowe Arms Hotel seem positively luxurious, I played "Twenty Questions" with a stern-looking bobby. Then Wiggs came in with a gleam in his eye. He was positively jolly!

"Like to stay with us a bit longer?" he asked.

"No, thanks."

"We can't detain you officially, of course."

"Which means you haven't believed a single word I've said. Is that it?" I asked bitterly.

"Wouldn't say that altogether, now. Actually there's someone we want you to meet, who may have a special bearing on the case. Unfortunately he's not available right now." He looked at his watch. "How about lunch on the house while you wait? We've got a pretty fair cook and I seem to remember you didn't get much in the way of breakfast."

"Who's coming?" I asked irritably.

Wiggs wagged an almost jocular finger. "You wait and see." Then he threw down an electric shaver on the table. "You might like to try this out. We keep it by us when we have to work all night."

A shave and lunch made me feel a lot better. It was a suspiciously good lunch, fitting admirably the condemned man's allegedly hearty breakfast. I ate alone, but if I wanted seconds, there was a bobby sitting outside the door, pretending it just happened to be his favourite seat and going mauve in the heavy draught from the outside door.

There was also a telephone on the table beside me.

I looked at it. Better tell Tom I was back again. There was no reply. He'd be off to Dinosaur Valley again, hating those red, white and blue decorations like hell, no thrill of a Royal visit for Tom, just the funeral wreaths for everything he loved.

I had an unhappy guilty feeling that I'd failed. Somewhere along the line. I ought to have sat down and given more time to the problem of Tom. As I replaced the receiver, I was nervously twisting a scrap of paper between my fingers.

V.B.421.

137

Strange that Wiggs should identify it immediately as the Rowe Vale Private Clinic. My heart began to beat wildly. Why hadn't I thought of that before?

What if Laurel was being kept prisoner? What more likely place to conceal her than in a mental hospital where patients normally made extravagant claims? They probably had everyone from Napoleon to Cleopatra. Even if she escaped temporarily, someone claiming to be Laurel Marsden-Smith in that set-up would be hardly worth the lift of an eyebrow. Just a wee thing barmy, that's all.

What better name to give her than Lorna Blagdon, an out-of-work schizophrenic actress, whose dreams of grandeur included being an heiress. Lorna Bladgon, who was nicely, safely, dead.

I dialled V.B.421. "May I speak to Miss Lorna Blagdon please?"

There was a moment's hesitation. "Wait please, caller."

I could hardly believe my good fortune. Then as time passed, I realised something had gone wrong. Footsteps approached the telephone. A murmured conversation, then a man's voice asked: "Whom do you want, please?"

"Miss Lorna Blagdon. I believe she's a patient with you."

"What is your name?"

"Brown – I'm er – a friend of hers."

"I'm sorry Mr. Brown, I'm afraid you've been misinformed. There is no one of that name here."

Replacing the receiver, I wondered why, if Lorna Blagdon wasn't there, the receptionist didn't say so immediately, as she did when once before I asked for "Victor"? Why the delay, the second opinion? And why had the doctor spoken at all, except to find out if I knew the password?

Wiggs came in and quickly I told him about the telephone call and what I suspected. He didn't seem surprised and I

138

wondered uncharitably if the telephone sitting there, so innocent, was tapped.

Behind Wiggs hovered a tall thin man, with thick glasses and a prominent Adam's apple. "Mr. MacGregor, this is Dr. Moore, he's the police psychiatrist. Now, now – don't blow your top!" I had already flashed to the door, bristling with fury at being tricked.

"You're not being tricked," said Dr. Moore smoothly. "As a matter of fact, Wiggs here thinks you're an extremely well-balanced young man."

"Bully for Wiggs! It's the first I've heard of it. Well, thanks for the lunch and the close shave. I'll get the brain-washing later, after I've found Laurel – if she's still alive!"

Wiggs said, "You daft young bugger!" and even the doctor looked shocked. "Don't you realise we're trying to help you. If this story of yours is true, you're going to need help. Just answer the doctor's questions, then you can go – pronto!"

The questions seemed pointless and merely inquisitive. Background, relations with my brother. Any other family? When did my parents die? Had I much sex life? Any special reasons for staying single so long then marrying so quickly? He finished with the old trick of suggesting objects whilst, angry and impatient to be away, I supplied what they conjured up for me. He seemed pleased. Did I suffer from headaches? Who was my doctor?

"Look, I've got to go. I'd like to be on hand before someone decides to shut up my wife for ever."

Picking up the telephone, he dialled the number with a pencil. With the receiver cradled beneath his chin, he smiled. "Won't take a moment. Hello? Fellton? This is Moore – yes, Moore. I'm fine. Yes, they're fine too. Doug starts at University next year. Isn't it amazing? Uh-hum. Yes. I've got one of your short-term patients here. Gregor MacGregor. You know him. He was! Well,

139

well." Moore looked across at me and had the audacity to wink. "Just about confirms my own diagnosis. Definitely – oh, yes, definitely. Yes, yes, I'll get him on to someone in Scotland. Nice to hear you. Must have that round of golf. How's the handicap? Ex-cell-ent! Cheerio!"

"What the hell do you think you're doing?" I demanded angrily. "I want to see Inspector Wiggs. Right now!"

Moore tapped his pencil thoughtfully. "Dr. Fellton confirms that you've been behaving in a singularly unbalanced way."

"Bastard!" I said violently.

He clucked his tongue disapprovingly. "Now, now! Let me continue. Apparently you drank too much and were abusive at the Rowe's house recently."

"I was drugged, you mean."

"Listen! Are you in a hurry to get back to Scotland?"

"You know damn well I'm not going anywhere until I find out what's happened to Laurel."

His eyes glistened behind the thick glasses. He looked oddly pleased. "Well, then, how would you like to go into the Rowe Vale Private Clinic? As a voluntary patient?"

"You mean that!"

He nodded. "My dear boy, I can't find anything wrong with you, except this obsessional neuroses about your wife. If it's true, all you've told me and Inspector Wiggs, then it's a natural enough mental state. The solution seems to be for you to go to the hospital and keep your eyes open. If she's being kept prisoner there, as you seem to think, well then – naturally we'd be interested. There's a lot of money at stake, you know."

"I don't care about the rotten money." I said savagely.

He help up a protesting hand. "All right, all right. I know, it's love or nothing." A moment later he was on the telephone to the doctor in charge of admitting patients at Rowe Vale (County Council Division). Half-an-hour later I was on my way.

PART THREE

See how love and murder will out.
(Congreve: The Double Dealer)

CHAPTER ONE

Leaving the police station, I walked into the heart of Rowe's Vale, already knee-deep in flags and bunting, bought some toilet articles and a heavy dark sweater. If I were going to prowl about in the middle of the night, a lounge suit and crumpled white shirt, already curling at the collar, like a dog-eared sandwich, were hardly practicable.

With my carrier bag, I swiftly covered the remaining distance to the flat. I was none-too-subtly being followed. However, the presence of that burly figure occupying the middle distance was strangely comforting. So obviously a bobby!

As the flat drew nearer, I consciously lessened the distance between us. Rowe must know that his sworn enemy was back in town and I felt as vulnerable as that point in all Westerns where the streets suddenly empty, and two men walk slowly towards each other.

Only I didn't feel that brave, just small and insignificant, a man who has strayed on to a drama much too big for him, quite by accident. If it hadn't been for Laurel, I would have turned and ran.

If the flat was being watched, it was in the hands of experts. Perhaps Rowe felt that with Wiggs on the job, there was no need to overdo things. Anyway, after shoving my new possessions into a discarded knapsack, impregnated with the smell of turps and linseed, I looked round feeling oddly disturbed by Tom's absence. I had this load of guilt for the sad old man. Despite my big words and bigger intentions, I hadn't been much use as comforter or friend, since I dragged him away from his beloved valley, promising so much.

As I left the flat, Wiggs materialised driving an unmarked car. I was humbly grateful, hardly desiring a spectacular arrival at the Rowe Vale Private Clinic, plus police escort, and looking like the prospective candidate for a strait jacket.

Wiggs drove silently along roads thick with patriotic symbols. Crowns and draped photographs precariously balanced, flags sprouting everywhere. I closed my eyes wearily. These damned flags only added to the poignancy of Tom's betrayal. Only a couple more days, then the first stage of the Rowe's Vale Dam would be under-way. Even away from the city centre there was the suppressed excitement, and the good humour, that foreshadows a Royal occasion. Every babe in its pram would be sucking on the stick-end of a Union Jack.

Wiggs was comfortably chewing his moustache and eyeing the decorations warily, hoping it would all go without incident, especially (he said) since the local force was so small they would have to get reinforcements from the County.

"Most likely the roads will be congested and that Civic Centre was never intended for the sight-seers who'll pile in from miles away. That car-park too! Couple of buses and half-a-dozen cars," he grumbled. "It's all right for you arty-crafty lads, with your fancy ideas, all tortured bits and pieces with a few trees thrown in. Give me the Romans any day. They knew how to build and how to make their roads too – straight as dies!"

"The Royal lunch will have to be in the Rowe canteen after all. Can you imagine them all tucked away in candle-lit corners at the Rowe Arms?" chortled Wiggs. "You can always change your mind and be present. Bask in a bit of glory as artist-in-chief."

"No, thanks," I said shortly. "Hope the sight of all that unleashed muscle and girth doesn't ruin the Royal appetite as much as it did mine."

"Tut, tut," said Wiggs, not unsympathetically, as we passed the ornate lodge gates, where one day, long ago, I had waved goodbye to a girl with silver fair hair, clutching a yellow pup in her arms. A girl like a princess from out of a fairy tale.

"It's a dashed good painting, you know, MacGregor. Something you'll feel proud of in another ten years. You just come back and look at it then. You'll feel better about a lot of things too, I'll bet. . . . Hold on! What the devil's happening here?"

There was a man in the middle of the road frantically waving a red flag. Wiggs reeled down the window. "What's up?"

"They're detonating now, sir. In the valley. You'll have to wait a while."

"Oh, yes, of course." Wiggs looked at his watch. "I'd forgotten. Dead on time too."

There was a violent explosion and the earth reverberated beneath us.

"That'll be the houses away," said Wiggs.

"Poor Tom Markham! This'll break his heart."

Seconds later it was over, and the man with the flag waved us on. I couldn't see into the valley from the car, but there was a small crowd of workmen and some furious-looking policemen grappled with a man. A man in a threadbare overcoat which was all too familiar.

"It's Tom!" And Wiggs stopped the car.

I dashed out. "Tom – what's wrong? What's happened?"

He stopped struggling and cursing, and turned to me. The tears poured down his cheeks unchecked, and dribbled into the deep hollows of his face. Oh, Tom!

He pointed a trembling hand down into the valley. Only two houses remained. Tom's house with its sundial and

145

slightly behind it, another smaller outhouse and an old barn. The house looked shocked and pitiful, surrounded by debris, with its satellite buildings, giving an illusion of doomed creatures shrinking close together for protection. It was weird and uncanny.

"Tom, I'm sorry," I said, quite inadequately. He stared at me, lost and bewildered, as if the words were spoken in an alien language. It was a look that reproached me for betraying him, for pretending help that was beyond giving, for absorption with my own affairs leaving no place for him. I had been his last hope and the glance that took in Wiggs and the car said I had deliberately cheated and gone over to the enemy, behaving like a typical product of my generation. The police constables seemed delighted to pass the buck to Wiggs. "What shall we do, sir? He was going to dash back into the house. Had to bring him out forcibly."

Wiggs watched the desolate valley and the desolate old man with the tear-streaked cheeks. "Come on, now, Tom. I'll tell you what we'll do. If you promise to be sensible and come away, we'll leave your house just as it is. Will that make you happy?"

"Can you do that?" asked Tom, uncertain of the magnitude of the reprieve being offered.

"It'll be all right, won't it – if you have my authority?" said Wiggs to the worried-looking foreman.

"Well, it was Mr. Rowe's orders, but if you say so," the man replied doubtfully, not wishing to antagonise the law. He looked down at the house and the outbuildings. Watching us, it seemed, waiting! "Can't see what harm it'll do to leave them, water'll cover them soon enough." He leaned over confidentially. "Beats me how the old man got in at all. We searched all the houses earlier, and there was no one in them then."

I looked at Tom, who had forgotten us, as he stared vacantly at his beloved house like a man with an ancient

146

dog to be imminently handed over to the final mercies of the vet.

Wiggs said, "I expect he has all sorts of secret ways in and out. After ninety years, it would be surprising if he didn't know a thing or two about the valley, wouldn't it?" He turned to the policemen. "Give him a lift home, will you? See he gets there safely, and get him something warm to drink on the way. Looks half-frozen, poor devil!" He walked over to Tom, and put his hand briefly on his shoulder, a wordless gesture of comfort. "Get away home, Tom. Your house will be all right, I promise you."

Tom said, "Aren't you coming back to the flat, Gregor?" If only I could have gone with him, done something for him for a change. "Why didn't you go back to Scotland with your brother?"

"I'll be going back soon. Look after the flat for me." He just stared, so forlorn and bewildered, that I wasn't sure whether he understood anything any more. As he went over to the police car, trailing his legs, stumbling, he turned at the door. His face had changed, it had that hard bright intensity as if there was something it was imperative to say.

"What is it, Tom?" I asked.

Then he shrugged, the light faded, and the saurian eyelids dropped. "Just goodbye, Gregor."

"Not goodbye," I said with false heartiness, "I'll be back in a day or two."

He shrugged, and climbed into the car.

As I sat down dejectedly beside Wiggs, I hoped he wasn't going to give me all that guff about progress, about the past making way.

All he said was, "Damned shame, isn't it? Makes you feel like a criminal taking the poor old beggar's home from him." Wrapped in our companionable share of guilt and gloom, we didn't say another word until at the entrance to the Rowe's Vale Private Clinic, Wiggs handed me the paint-spattered knapsack. "You can still change your mind, MacGregor. We're not forcing you into this."

I shook my head. If only I could find Laurel. Together we could help Tom rebuild his life. It was as though there was an enormous sandglass in the back of my mind gradually, stealthily, trickling away.

"Thanks for everything," I said to Wiggs. He held out his hand. "We'll be looking out for you. Good luck, MacGregor."

CHAPTER TWO

Homely ivy shrouded the Clinic's walls. With a flower-bedded drive leading up to the front door, it looked like many other Victorian homes of the manorial class, built with a kind of determined understatement, so typical of the stiff upper lips that fought the Crimean War.

The interior was like stepping into another world. Tiled floors with a scattering of pleasantly-shaped modern chairs and low tables, the décor cheerfully, but gently, artistic. It was rather more students' hostel than hospital, except for a service department of uniformed nurses, some of them pushing rather antiseptic-looking rubber-wheeled trolleys. Dr. Moore had been efficient, too.

Immediately I gave my name, the pretty receptionist I had spoken to previously on the telephone, had me through to Dr. Folkes, the registrar. A tall thin man, with an immense brow and more teeth gathered together in one mouth, than I would have thought possible for someone who wasn't a crocodile, he checked my name and address, said Dr. Moore had requested my admission. Was that right? And that was all.

He personally escorted me to a small but pleasant room on the ground floor, which I noted thankfully, visualising some nocturnal ramblings where it would be just my luck to have a third-floor room. I soon gathered that referring to illness was considered the grossest bad taste.

The window of my room looked over lawns towards a more modern wing, not visible from the front of the house. "There's a library," said Dr. Folkes, "you can order your papers, and within reason, what you prefer to eat. If you have any hobby, you can arrange to do it," he laughed heartily, "as long as it isn't too big, or too noisy of course. We like to feel that our visitors enjoy some sort of occupational therapy. It's so restful for them."

He pointed to a bell on the wall. "And please remember, we are all at your service, everyone here is your friend. If you have er-problems, any need to talk to someone – day or night – you just have to press that bell." He looked at his watch. "You'll get dinner in an hour and meet some of the other visitors. Don't be shy or afraid to talk to them. Everyone is most friendly and willing to co-operate." With a rallying flash of splendid white teeth, he was gone.

It seemed all too good to be true, and having a natural distrust of perpetrators of sweetness and light, I waited about thirty seconds then cautiously tried the door handle.

Contrary to my nasty suspicions, it was unlocked. So were the windows. They worked smoothly and silently and I could step over that sill on the lawn at any time, which might have considerable advantages.

Freedom apparently extended beyond the room, too. I was free to go anywhere, receiving nothing but kind looks on my exploratory journey, plus some beaming smiles from the nurses.

At the unspectacular, but adequate, meal which followed in the television room ("for those who preferred company," said Dr. Folkes), I met several more "visitors". Two of them seemed old established customer playing their nightly game of chess, like a pair of elderly business men who had never suffered worse than an attack of indigestion.

There were others whose oddness was silence and who retreated immediately the meal was over. A young fellow wearing a dressing-gown and a faraway smile remained.

I was glad to escape. In the corridor several men stood smoking and talking. They had presumably eaten in their rooms. But as far as I could see, no one was locked in.

My hopes of Laurel began to fade. How could anyone conceal an unwilling prisoner in a set-up like this?

On the way to my room, I chatted to a nurse pushing a trolley. "Are there many of us here?"

She said yes.

"All men?" I asked. She laughed and gave me a coy look. "No, the ladies have a separate establishment." Ah, how I loved that careful language! Nothing so bawdy as "ward", or "warder", or "hospital". Whoever designed the language must have bordered on genius.

"You're in a room which faces the lawns? Well, you can see the other establishment from the window. Sir Arthur Marsden-Smith donated that wing and enlarged the back premises when we – er – amalgamated with Rowe's."

It was the wing I had observed earlier, certainly looking innocent enough with ladies, who I had taken for off-duty nurses, sitting in the open windows.

"Do you have anyone locked in? Away from the rest, I mean." I hated to sound so crude, but the information was vital.

The nurse stared at me. "Good heavens, no! What an extraordinary idea! Everyone is quite free. You could walk out right this moment if you wished, and no one would even try to stop you!" she said stiffly, then relenting at my solemn face, asked: "Will you be having visitors this evening?"

"No. I thought I might take a stroll – out in the grounds."

"By all means. Lights are out at nine, but you can read in your own room after that."

My next move was to investigate any entrance common to both "establishments." But making my way along a series of windowed corridors, I always reached a dead end. The house was apparently completely divided into two parts.

It was dark now, so guided by the lights shining from the ladies' wing, I decided to go visiting. I donned an abominable deer-stalker hat dredged up from the depths of the knapsack. Bought in a weak moment for painting outside, and suffering lamentably from exposure to linseed, turps, plus a general disinclination to wear it, it seemed to offer some measure of disguise.

From the terrace, dark silhouettes of trees moved eerily on the drive and making sure that I was unobserved, I loped over the garden and stood panting near the entrance to the other wing, feeling ridiculously like Sylvester stalking Tweetypie.

From behind a tree, I watched the visitors' visitors plodding up the steps and, deciding that I was underclad, teetered off into the flower-beds where I picked a generous bunch. Putting on an unseasonably dark pair of sunglasses, which reduced my vision to nil, I stumbled up the front steps. Into the reception lobby I shrank my seventy-two inches as unobtrusively as possible amongst the other visitors.

What if someone asked me who I visited? What then?

The bell clanged and, like a nervous horse, I bolted down the nearest corridor. There were no names on the doors, but by the cheerful rattle of crockery, I knew I was in the kitchen regions. Hurriedly backtracking down a corridor to the left, I surprised several patients who were visitorless and unprepared for a human thunderbolt travelling past.

Taking off my glasses I had to admit I was lost. A girl in a dressing-gown trudged past carry a book. "Can you tell me which is Miss Lorna Blagdon's room?" I asked.

She looked abominably scared and clutching the neck

of her gown wildly, said in a voice of doom, "I'm sorry, you'd better ask someone else."

By dint of pocketing my glasses, I discovered that the doors down the next corridor had numbers on them. Taking one at random, I knocked gently. There was a light step inside and a middle-aged lady appeared. I was obviously not the visitor she expected, for disappointment wreathed her face.

"I'm looking for Miss Blagdon. Miss Lorna Blagdon?"

She shook her head, obviously displeased that I wasn't whoever she expected. "I've no idea who she might be. Why don't you ask a nurse?" And before I could stop her, she shouted. "Nurse – here, nu –rse! He wants Miss – what-did-you-say – Blagdon, was it?"

The nurse had grey hair and a face to match. She wore old-fashioned steel-rimmed specs, and behind them her ferocious expression suggested that her feet might be giving her hell. "Who is it you want?" she asked briskly.

"Miss Lorna Blagdon."

A very blank and cautious "Oh!" was the reply.

"I seem to have lost my way," I said awkwardly, screwing out a nonchalant smile.

"Are you expected?"

"Yes – I think so."

"I don't know the number off-hand." There was a curious penetrating look. "Better go back to reception. Come along, I'll take you."

"Don't trouble . I know the way – straight back and to the right." As I walked away, twice I turned and she was still watching. Just making, sure that I didn't unwittingly stumble on something indiscreet perhaps?

The reception desk was empty and to cool the nurse's suspicions, I devoted a careful study to the notices on the board. Making sure she had gone, I turned to continue the search and there, on top of the empty desk, was a list. Cautiously turning it round, I examined it

153

carefully, leaning idly on the desk as if waiting for someone.

The first two floors contained twenty rooms, each, occupied and accounted for. On the third floor only three rooms were taken – 41, 42, 43. There was a long gap then a room 49.

It was marked simply "X".

CHAPTER THREE

The receptionist returned, talking to one of the visitors. I busied myself with the notice board, absorbed in the instructions to nurses on regulation uniform. Then I meandered across to the stairs, pausing at an alcove to dump my flowers in a large bowl, already fully occupied by some of their chums. How beautifully they matched, almost as if they had come from the same plot!

There was no one around and I took the stairs two at a time. There wasn't much of the visiting hour left and to be caught loitering afterwards, as well as doing untold damage to my reputation, would have consequences little short of hair-raising!

A fox on the rampage in a battery of hens would have a quieter reception. I would be lucky if I wasn't drummed out of the Clinic and presented to Wiggs on a charge of rape and assault!

Well, so far so good. I had shot up two flights of stairs without anyone asking embarrasing questions. At the top of the third staircase, the rooms and corridor looked smaller and less impressive – like the kind of hotel room I frequently landed by asking "Have you anything cheaper?" I was willing to bet the view from the windows consisted of large areas of drain-pipe and red-brick, and that the stillness of the night was shattered by the sounds of plumbing.

After the cheerful lighting below, this corridor was illuminated with an economy that would have gladdened Callum's heart.

The rooms numbered 41, 42, 43, had strips of light showing. The others were dark until 49. It also had a light, one of those red ghostly hospital night-lights, which shone through the fanlight.

Cautiously, I turned the handle.

The door was locked. In this place of ever-open doors, it gave a nasty jolt, like finding out that one's favourite aunt has some unspeakable vices. I tried again, then giving it a wee tap, I said:

"Laurel? Laurel, are you there?"

There was no reply and I was bracing myself for another clarion call when there were footsteps on the stair.

Clear-thinking at such moments was not my speciality. There was a door opposite and I flung myself in blindly, expecting at best to hear the night cleft by outraged female screams. Instead I was overwhelmed by the smell of camphor, nicely blended and sustained with antiseptic.

Deciding I was the last person with whom I cared to share a linen cupboard, I peered out cautiously, heard the nurse's voice back down the hall and throwing dignity to the winds, did the Sylvester caper and was rushing headlong downstairs just as the departure bell sounded.

The more I thought about that locked room, the surer I was that if – a very big "if" – Laurel was a prisoner, that's where she was hidden. No freedom for her! What in God's name did they expect to do with her? They could hardly hide her for ever? Or, a still cold voice inside me suggested, were they taking care of that too, perhaps slow poison or a steady overdose of drugs?

There was another urgent question. Supposing I was right! Supposing I got in and found her, how the devil was I going to get her out again? I didn't see myself as Superman, fending off villains with one hand and some accurately directed foul-play, whilst fighting my way to the exit with Laurel tucked under my other arm, (in all probability bung full of drugs and sleeping pills).

156

It was ten o'clock. Back in my room I was being offered something to drink. I had a moment's hope, until I surveyed hot milk and drinks basically consisting of more hot milk. I longed for whisky – a great big bottle of it!

By midnight I was bursting with impatience. I would have gone back to the other wing and beaten all the doors down, except that – for all the deceptive attitudes of everyone being on Scouts honour and all free as dickey-birds – I expected a certain amount of stringent observation during the hours of darkness in the ladies' department, particularly when the boys next-door were well-known not to have all their buttons on. Someone might decide in the middle of the night that he was a dissatisfied King Solomon on the rampage for more wives.

Well I wasn't going to play the rash intruding fool. I'd wait until daylight and have a shot at Room X, armed with some low cunning, and precious little else by the looks of it. It was a little late to bewail the fact that I might have spent time profitably mastering something deadlier than a paintbrush.

The night was endless, a little hell of time going backwards, with morning eternally frustrated. When, at eighty-thirty, the nurse brought breakfast, she said, "My, but you are up with the larks!"

"I thought I'd take a stroll in the grounds," and sniffing the air like a restive stag, "It's a grand morning."

"It is indeed," and indicating the books I carried, "I think you'll find it too chilly to read in the garden though. Now don't catch cold. Here, come back and have your breakfast first," she added in mock stern tones.

I gulped down toast and tea whilst she made the bed. Then putting on my sheepskin jacket, I bounded over the lawns, making my approach look as near as possible from the direction of the drive.

The receptionist was busy with the telephone. Cleaners noisily vacuumed the lobby and, whistling cheerfully like a fledgling doctor with a fascinating tonsilectomy to perform, I bustled my way up to the third floor.

The corridor was deserted except for a depressed-looking wardmaid, humping blankets out of the cupboard where I had hidden last night.

"Hello, dear," I said in my heartiest young doctor voice and boldly tried the handle of the room marked "X". "What's wrong? Seems to be locked. Any idea where the key is?" I tapped the books. "Doc Fellton wants her to have these."

The wardmaid had big sad eyes, their blue all washed out, as if she occasionally threw them into the washing machine along with the dirty linen. She said dully, "Nurse keeps that key herself. She'll be at her breakfast, I expect."

"Oh, damn!" I said, and meant it.

She looked down the corridor then furtively shoved over a bunch of keys. "Here, try that one! It's for emergencies. Fits any of the doors, I expect."

"Oh, ta, ever so! That'll do the trick."

It did. The lock turned soundlessly.

Now I was in trouble again. With my hand on the doorknob, for a large number of reasons, I didn't want to open the door before the eyes of the curious wardmaid. What if it wasn't Laurel at all?

I need not have feared. Snatching the bunch of keys back, she said nervously, "You'd better watch yourself. She's one of the violent ones. Here – don't open it yet – I'm off!" And she hurried down the corridor without a backward glance.

Next to the linen cupboard, I had noticed a laundry room. Keeping a wary eye on the door of room "X", I took twenty seconds to find what I wanted, roll it under my coat and taking a big, deep breath I took a grip on the door handle.

The possibility of Laurel being inside had never seemed

more remote. What if I opened the door and some crazy old girl like Mr. Rochester's mad wife, went charging down the corridor on the rampage with a breadknife?

And if Laurel wasn't there – where, in God's name – could I look next? What if the whole crazy pattern *was* wrong, and Laurel had only pretended to love me and then had died in the road accident outside the Rowe Arms. And Lorna Blagdon, large as life, was enjoying Majorca and some illicit love with her rich protector.

Well, there was only one way to find out. Slowly I opened the door.

The room was dim and "X" had her back towards me. She sat by the window and her hands hung limply over the sides of the chair. It was an attitude of shattering hopelessness and despair.

She moved slightly when the door opened fully.

"Please go away! Please, please leave me alone!"

The voice was quite unmistakeable.

CHAPTER FOUR

"Laurel!"

She turned and a moment later, weak as she was, she flung herself into my arms.

"Oh, Greg!" she sobbed. "I knew you'd come! I knew you'd find me. Oh, Greg!" She wasn't particularly coherent, and neither was I, looking down on the silvery-fair hair, now neglected and untidy. The pale face was pinched with cold and suffering, somehow making the surprisingly dark eyebrows and the deep blue eyes stand out more vividly than ever.

But this was Laurel! Unmistakably the Laurel I had loved and married. Now I remembered the other one, the coarseness of skin hidden by heavy make-up, the look of worldliness and experience that no plastic surgery could hide. But because love is blind as a bat in a coal cellar, because I had wanted her to be Laurel, I had accepted the substitute. Only the deeper senses had been troubled and offended by my blindness. All the subtleties that go to make attraction, the very individual smell of hair and skin and sweat that make up the intangible chemical substance of love had been missing. And no plastic surgery could give a girl who had heavier bones and features, and weighed nearly a stone more, the fragility of Laurel.

She was crying softly, clinging as if she was scared I would vanish again. "They told me you'd gone away. That they paid you five thousand pounds and you agreed to forget the whole thing. Oh, darling, will you ever forgive me for believing it?" Her hands tightened. "Listen!"

160

We both looked at the door. There were sounds in the corridor.

The dangerous world that awaited outside this room, and the avalanche about to crash down on us, were back again. Perhaps the sinister reality never seemed so ominous and inescapable as in this brief lovers' meeting. I had found her again! I had believed her dead and gone. Now here she was, miraculously alive, breathing warmly in my face, loving and real.

All I had to do was to get her away. Only I hadn't the faintest idea how we'd manage to the front door, much less to Rowe's Vale and the protection of Inspector Wiggs.

Rowe must know I was here, that I suspected Laurel was alive. What was surprising was that they had let me get this far. It had all seemed remarkably easy. Perhaps escape would be easy too. Except for one solemn, deadly thing – this would be a fight to the death whoever won. Hartley Rowe couldn't afford to let either of us live now.

Outside the door, the sound of footsteps died away.

"Come on, let's go," I said. "We'll get away, don't worry!" marvelling at the glib conviction I certainly did not feel, "Where's your coat?"

"I haven't one – nothing but what I'm wearing." She had on the fine cashmere sweater and tweed skirt she had worn on our first meeting in Dinosaur Valley, now looking sadly limp and past its best. It had fitted her then, emphasising her slender exquisite body. Now it merely hung on her bones.

"You must be frozen in that!"

She smiled. "They took my coat away, and when I asked them for more clothes they said I could wrap in a blanket if I was cold." She shivered, leaning closer. "Do you know, Greg, sometimes I would have signed away every penny of the Rowe fortune just to be warm again, just to roast myself in front of a fire for ten minutes. I've never – been – so cold."

161

"Oh, darling! Can you bear to be cold for just a few minutes longer, until we get out of here?" I handed her the nurse's dress, apron and cap I had lifted from the laundry room. "Put these on!"

My mind was way ahead, already walking down the stairs, walking the "nurse" past the reception desk, through the lobby, out of the front door, down the drive to the main road. Hardly a flourishing highway, but perhaps with more traffic because of the Royal visit, we'd be lucky and get a lift. Perhaps Laurel's "uniform" would be an asset, too, for lorry drivers are not always keen to stop, particularly when there had been an outburst of lurid hold-ups lately.

Laurel was stripping off the sweater and skirt, and I cursed Hartley Rowe and promised to settle another score. By God! They must have been starving her to death. She was so frail she could hardly stand without help.

"Did they not feed you?" I asked angrily.

"Well, at first I never wanted anything. I was so miserable and angry. I had some idea that if I went on a hunger strike they'd have to let me go, that they couldn't afford to let me die." She shrugged. "After a while I realised that keeping me alive wasn't part of the plan, so I ate what they brought, which wasn't much." Then she added surprisingly, "I've starved before, you know – long ago. Once your stomach shrinks it's almost bearable." (That must have been the first time, when she was kidnapped as a child). "I suppose I must be doped, I sleep most of the time."

She looked weary and exhausted. No wonder it had all seemed so easy once I set foot into the Clinic. Now it seemed ominously easy. She was like someone suffering from a hangover who just wanted to get her head down. Even the effort of dressing had taxed her unutterably.

How in Heaven's name, were we going to get away? What if we had to hide out for a while? She would need all her strength, and wits too. In this weather it would be tough going on someone of Eva's stamina, but for this frail doll-like creature, it would be certain death.

It looked grimly as if Rowe had foreseen the whole thing, as rubbing his white hands together, he cast me in the role of Laurel's executioner!

Impatiently I helped her button the neck of the dress, she was agonisingly slow and her hands were like ice.

I opened the door and looked out. Our luck had faded too. There was a maid down on her knees scrubbing the corridor.

"Wait until she's past this door, then we can go out. I've never seen any of the nurses, except one, so they won't recognise me like this," said Laurel.

It seemed a risky business. "All these delays!" I grumbled.

She smiled at me. "Be patient, darling, it's just a few minutes more. I've waited weeks just for you to come. What month is it, anyway, I came here at the end of October?"

I told her we were into December now.

"They brought me from London. Dr. Fellton said Mother would have to stay for a few days' observation and that I was to go back to Rowe's Vale with them next day. I was scared for Mother. I thought it was a relapse. He gave me a couple of pills. I woke up in Rowe House. Then Lorna arrived. I was so glad to see her!"

Her face brightened at the memory, then remembering the disillusion that swiftly followed, she said sadly. "She told me Mother was dead. She'd had an accident, but if I was a good girl and did as Vic Fellton said, she would see that no one harmed me. She said Uncle Hartley was in trouble, he needed Mother's money for a while. The firm was just a hollow mockery and he and Vic Fellton might go to prison. She said I wouldn't want that to happen, would I, when she and Vic were getting married.

163

"I wanted her to stay – made a terrible fuss about her going. Next time she came, I told her about you, about getting married, and she was terribly angry and frightened. I wondered why she looked so like me, like the photographs we had taken long ago. She said it was to help Vic, by pretending to be me. And I knew she was in it too.

I never saw her again – I don't think I wanted to any more after that. A few days later they brought me here." she paused. "Where is she now?"

"She's dead," I said brutally. "In a street accident."

Laurel shuddered. "Poor Lorna."

I said angrily, "Poor Lorna, indeed! She was almost party to your murder and she certainly helped kill your mother, if not literally, at least by being an accessory."

She looked at me sadly. "I know, Greg, but I'm still sorry for her. She wanted so much out of life and when she got it, whether it was money, or fame, or love, it never lasted. She used to cry, 'Always, it always turns to ashes for me!'."

"Does Fellton come and see you?"

"No. Just an elderly grey-haired dragon of a nurse."

"Does she wear old-fashioned steel-rimmed specs?"

Laurel said yes.

"I think I met her yesterday," I groaned.

"I'm a special case, a schizophrenic – dangerous some-times, that's why I'm locked up." She paused. "I wonder what they've got in mind. You know I keep waiting, knowing when it happens, it'll be terrible. I once saw a thing about concentration camps. It horrified me so that I used to have a dream. Watching my friends disappear one by one to the gas chambers and wondering when it would be my turn. Every time the door opened, I'd think: This is it! It's like that now, only there isn't anyone left but me."

The blue eyes were candid and terrible. "You must

have thought of that, Greg. They can't afford to keep me here indefinitely. What if someone was careless and I escaped?"

I opened the door. The maid was scrubbing far past the door, down on her knees, with her back towards us.

("What if someone was careless and I escaped?" Laurel had said.)

We found the answer to that one much earlier than we expected. And with it the answer to why it had all been so easy to get to Laurel. Too damned easy!

Hartley Rowe, with his passion for the well-turned cliché, would have nailed this one exactly, as "Killing two birds with one stone!"

CHAPTER FIVE

Taking a deep breath, I walked out of Laurel's prison, hoping my harrassed expression would add weight to the young and eager doctor role. A few paces behind came Laurel, all her hair pushed under a cap and her head lowered behind a pile of bedding. I bundled her sweater and skirt under my jacket for use later. The only thing I couldn't fix at short notice, were her light shoes and nylons.

Before we reached the first landing, I had filched a temperature chart from a stationary trolley and I was beginning to feel we might manage the whole journey without incident. Then, two nurses, coming along the corridor, nudged each other and said to Laurel:

"Hey, nurse! You new here?"

Laurel murmured yes. The elder nurse grinned. "Well, you'd better get into your uniform shoes and stockings fast. Don't tell me you haven't read the notices about being improperly dressed!"

"No," whispered Laurel.

"You'll be sorry you didn't! Matron's on the warpath and Sister'll give you hell for nylons and those stiletto heels."

"I'll go and change," said Laurel, looking frantic.

The nurses turned their attention on me as I lingered, obviously waiting and obviously impatient. God, the grey-haired nurse might turn that corner at any minute.

The younger one said cheekily. "No flirting with the

doctors either, nurse," and chortled as she hurried down the corridor.

Laurel swayed dangerously and her face was deathly pale. I gripped her elbow. "For God's sake keep going. We've lost enough time."

Stumbling, she followed me downstairs. The reception desk was empty, so was the lobby. Like an oasis stood the glass door. We were almost out.

Almost.

Laurel was staggering, panting with exertion and fatigue behind the small stack of linen. "Come on, darling, hurry! Just a few more steps."

We reached the door.

My hand was on the handle when trudging briskly up the steps, straight for us, came the burly form of Dr. Fellton.

We turned and from behind us, speedily negotiating the lobby, came Laurel's gimlet-eyed nurse. We were trapped. I looked at Laurel, wondering if I could pick her up and make a bolt for it. I looked at Fellton and changed my mind.

I know it sounds the height of melodrama to think of doctors flourishing wicked-looking revolvers in empty hospital lobbies, to persuade unwilling patients into ambulances, but there we stood like a bunch of paralysed rabbits. It was all so damned unreal, I wanted to laugh, waiting for Fellton's leering close-up to dissolve into captions before the play faded out.

Then I spotted the telephone.

Could I make a dash for it, get Wiggs dialled before Fellton overpowered me. Laurel wasn't much help there, for when I let go her arm, she just folded to the ground like a rag-doll with its saw-dust gone. What a time to faint!

Still covering me with the revolver, Fellton gathered her up like a spilt parcel and said, "You'd better come along without any fuss," and in a nasty voice added to the nurse,

"It's quite providential that I knew MacGregor had been admitted and thought I'd better check up on my patient."

"This – this man," blustered the nurse, blinking behind the steel-rimmed glasses and looking far from the formidable dragon of our last encounter. She was very frightened indeed, as well one who failed Rowe's might have cause to be. "This man – he – he – "

"I know all about him," said Fellton grimly, and he thrust Laurel on to her feet again, until she was cradled against his shoulder. It looked a touchingly amorous scene till you got a glance at his face.

"Don't try any more tricks," he advised and herded us over to the telephone on the desk. "Dial 211," he said to the nurse.

Shaking with terror she did so, and handed him the receiver in an ingratiating deprecatory manner, as if the fact that she did it so nicely might lessen the punishment coming her way.

"Hello," said Fellton, "Inspector Wiggs, please. MacGregor here. Yes, I'll hang on." He turned to me. "All right, MacGregor, say your piece nicely. It was a mistake, you've searched the place, Laurel isn't here and you've decided to go home tomorrow."

There was a squeak at the other end, and with a sibilant, "Any improvisations and Laurel dies," he thrust the instrument into my hand.

"MacGregor, that you?" came Wiggs' voice, crackling over the line.

"Yes." And I said my piece, hoping I sounded as stiff and unnatural as I felt, watching Fellton press the black muzzle of the revolver into Laurel's side.

Wiggs sounded puzzled and disappointed. "Ah, well, I suppose that's that. It was an interesting theory. Never mind," he said consolingly, "you did your best. We'll get in touch with you if we hear anything."

Fellton looked almost amiable as I replaced the receiver.

"'Phone the usual number for an ambulance, nurse, we'll wait in the car," and he led the way outside.

We passed a group of nurses teetering up the steps, giggling helplessly. They didn't give us a second glance. There was nothing unusual about Dr. Fellton, a nurse and a strange man making for a car.

I considered yelling at them and found Fellton watching grimly. "Save your breath, MacGregor. Lorna Blagdon is a violent patient, escaping with a crackpot from the men's department. I'm just humouring you both along until the ambulance comes."

The glass door swung closed behind the nurses.

We went into the back of the car, whilst Fellton unobtrusively covered us from the front. During this short wait, he "talked". He could afford that luxury, knowing what lay just a few hours ahead for us.

Several times, I toyed with the idea of rushing him, stealing the car, but I was such a proven bungler and certain now that he intended to kill us anyway, all I would do was make it an early certainty.

"What are you going to do with us?" asked Laurel with a kind of dulled indifference. "Let Gregor go, please – let him go! I'll do anything you say if you'll let him go! This has nothing to do with him."

The eau-de-nil eyes surveyed me. "Hasn't it, indeed? He's interfered plenty. Can you honestly see him going quietly home and leaving you now?" I looked at the handsome face, with the incongruous pale eyes beneath the black hair. The face of a movie idol rather than a born killer. I wondered.

"Don't plead for me, Laurel, we're in this together. I wouldn't dream of going and missing the fun now."

"How sensible," said Fellton drily.

"How did you get in with Rowe's thugs, anyway," I asked. "What's your cut out of all this?"

"Plenty," he said shortly. "And if you're going to give

me the dedicated doctor's devotion to humanity, you can save your breath."

I thought of the empty consulting room, the terror of the golf course, his alleged success with women. "I'd be surprised if you were a doctor at all."

"What do you mean? What do you know about it?" he demanded furiously.

My shot in the dark had slightly grazed his armour. I thought rapidly. "Hartley Rowe isn't going to get away with it. Inspector Wiggs is on to him, he had me planted at the Clinic to spy out the land."

Fellton winced and looked pale.

"It's just a question of time before they get you too. They've guessed about the porter's suit you stole. Look, you must know plenty about Rowe, why not save your neck whilst you have the chance?" Only a bullet would stop me now.

"Are you mad?" said Fellton shakily. "Turn against Hartley Rowe!" It jogged a disagreeable stream of memory. Eva saying "Against Rowe's?" in precisely the same tone. As if sacrilege, and desecration of sacred shrines had been suggested.

"You'll go to prison if you don't."

Fellton laughed. "I'll go to prison if I do." He momentarily considered our potential danger, decided it was non-existent, and continued. "A few years ago I was being blackmailed on account of I never qualified, and Hartley had my brilliant degrees forged. He helped me stage an accident- one of those unsolved hit-and-run affairs. However, he made sure of my price, sure that he had enough to hang me."

"What about Aunt Judith?" asked Laurel.

Fellton laughed bitterly. "That harpy. She'd sell our grandmother for a decent minkcoat."

In truly feminine fashion, Laurel asked, "Were you really going to marry Lorna?"

170

Fellton shook his head. "Of course not. After she served her purpose, Hartley had already decided she'd have to go."

"You don't think Lorna would have gone without a fight, do you? All her life had been a jungle – she had the tenacity of a tiger."

Fellton smiled. "I think you misunderstand me. When I said she would have to go, I meant silenced – permanently!" He let that sink in. "My dear girl," he added gently, "Don't waste your sympathy on Lorna. She was an ineffectual idiot, after the – er – unfortunate occurrence on the train, she was up to her elbows in murder."

"So Gregor was right!" cried Laurel.

"If it's any comfort to you, your mother had only a few years longer, the operation was a purely temporary matter. And if she had looked like lasting too long for Hartley's comfort, rest assured he would have found some way to expedite matters. However, to get back to Lorna, she found a handsome male so irresistible that once she talked to your charming Gregor here, she weakened and tried to warn him off. As an accomplice she had some very unreliable traits, falling into the arms of every presentable man who came along. Not one whit of staying-power or self-control!" He sighed. "In a way, her end was most providential, and so convenient too! Ah, this looks like the ambulance."

"Look!" said Laurel desperately, "If you hate Uncle Hartley so much, why help him at all? Let us escape and I'll give you money. All the money you want. You can go abroad!"

Fellton laughed. "Very generous of you, my dear. However, I'm not a naturally trusting character. I feel a damned lot safer with my somewhat insalubrious wagon hitched to Hartley's unscrupulous star, than to young lovers with moral principles."

The ambulance stopped alongside. Two grim looking

171

men emerged, their bulk, squashed faces and unbeautiful ears suggesting a marked earlier acquaintance with the inside of a boxing ring.

"You know what to do," said Fellton. They apparently knew.

We were thrust inside the ambulance and the doors locked behind us. It was a sturdily built vehicle, with thick frosted glass to keep in, or out, prying eyes. We might as well have been sealed into a salmon tin for all the hopes of escape it offered.

For the best part of an hour, there was a considerable amount of climbing and changing gears, and from the unpleasant swaying and grinding some negotiating of rather unfrequented tracks.

At last the engine stopped.

We looked at each other and waited.

CHAPTER SIX

The big ugly face of the driver motioned us outside.

It was a beautiful day for a murder.

We were high up on deserted moorland. At this time of year, with snowfall imminent, I hated to think how long our bodies would lie undiscovered. There was nothing but burnt-looking heather and a few curious sheep with nervous dispositions.

The long road we had climbed twisted wetly downwards to fold its lower reaches into dismal mist.

No one spoke. Our breath hung like four small balloons in the icy air. After a moment our companions added to this illusion by putting an enormous amount of energy into some ferocious chain-smoking.

When I said, "You haven't got a spare cigarette by any chance?" they both stared at me, then at each other, and decided to ignore it. I considered they were probably deaf mutes, chosen for that very reason.

We must have presented a delicious little quartet. Two great thugs, a tiny girl barely visible inside my sheepskin jacket, and myself, shivering miserably in elegant shirt and the trousers of my lounge suit.

Then the complete silence was broken by a distant sound. A car climbing, growing nearer.

My spirits rose as a small dark van climbed the hill. Our companions who had their back to it, hadn't batted an eyelid and as I was filling my lungs to scream for help, it slowed down beside us.

I should have known. This was what we had been waiting for. This was part two of the plan.

We were pushed unceremoniously inside by our charming friends, who decided they liked us so well that they would come along too, leaving the ambulance to be disposed of, by the driver of the van.

On we trundled. The van was less comfortable than our former transport and a howling gale came through a rather large crack in the doors. I was willing to bet the vehicle had been stolen earlier that day and the doors forced open.

Poor Laurel was so exhausted, and still so full of drugs and weakness, that she had fallen asleep. I made her as comfortable as I could and watched her anxiously, wondering if she had reached delirium, for she talked in her sleep about the lovely warm fire.

The pace was slow and bone-rattling, over some very unfrequented roads, and sitting there, chilled to the bone we were thrown all over the floor in the darkness! It would have been uncomfortable in a normal car. Well, it wasn't the worst part of the ordeal by any means, but then I was misguided and optomistic enough to believe it might well be.

The end of our mystery tour had me baffled. It was almost dark when we stopped and putting my eye to the crack in the door, I found we were back on the road to Rowe's Vale – about half-a-mile past Tom's valley.

In front no one moved. Laurel slept on, more peacefully now, and as the cracks of light diminished outside, so complete darkness came. There was a moderate amount of traffic on the road, and as occasional sweeps of light from headlamps caught us, I began to hope again.

I tried the doors, but they held firm. Then, in desperation, I began shouting and banging on the walls. It only brought the irate drivers to indicate, by some very explicit dumbshow, the prospect of Laurel being knocked about by them if I didn't subside, I subsided quick enough!

What were they waiting for, anyway? If this was the end of our journey, why didn't they kill us and get it over with?

Laurel was fully awake now and the same thought must have occurred to her, for she whispered, "Perhaps they're going to ship us abroad or something."

I would have vouched for the "something" personally, a less winsome, expensive and more permanent end!

Then she said the first word that gave a glimmer of hope. "You know, Greg, don't you, that I'd have a terrible job proving my identity in this country? Uncle Hartley certainly couldn't have planned it better. Living abroad most of my life. Going to school in Paris. By the time I grew up, Mother was too ill, anyway, to want to socialise, for the few weeks we were here each summer.

"What about servants when you were in Rowe House?"

"We had Aunt Judith's housekeeper. Now I understand why she looked scared when I tried to be friendly. She also engaged a couple of housemaids, whom we hardly saw at all."

"Very convenient! What about people in Rowe's Vale?" I asked desperately. "Did you ever see Inspector Wiggs?"

"The policeman on traffic duty was the nearest I ever got to the law." She thought for a moment. "Oh! There were a few shop assistants, a hairdresser – but don't you see, they have accepted Lorna in my place. My only friend, before you came along was Tom Markham. Poor old Tom."

"He'll be able to identify you."

She shook her head. "No, Greg. Who would take the word of an old man of ninety? A tiresome old man, a known troublemaker at Rowe's. They'd think it was pure spite. No, there's only one solution. We must get to Paris, I have friends there."

"Wait a minute! I met a fellow, when I was looking for you. Vincent Barnes. He knew you when you were small, did some alternations to the hot-water system at Rowe House."

Laurel laughed. "I remember him, a nice man who used to feed me jelly babies. I used to call him Barney."

"Well, we could get him."

She put her hand on my arm. "It's no *use*, Greg. You still don't see what we're up against, do you? It's one man's word against *Rowe's*. It isn't a Sunday School Uncle Hartley's running, he'll stop at nothing – bribery, ruin. The murder of one individual, well, he wouldn't consider that worth a second thought, or a moment's conscience, if it helped him add one more Van Gogh, one piece of Dresden china, to his collection.

"You're not dealing with a man who has moral values – or a conscience. He needed money – mine or my mother's." She paused grimly. "Well, if he can treat his relations like that, how would he treat a mere someone who worked for the firm?"

She was quiet after that and I thought she had fallen asleep. Then she said, "It's all my fault, darling. If I hadn't rushed you into marrying me, you'd be free – away in Scotland, and I'd be the fading memory of a girl you had dated a few times."

"That's not true, Laurel! I loved you from the first moment. I'd never forget you! You can't imagine the agony of believing you were just playing a game, that I was a rich girl's whim, as Lorna tried to pretend. Then having to believe you were dead. Gone for ever, crying for someone she called Vic, as she died."

Laurel thought for a moment. "Yes, I really did play into their hands. They must have planned this for years. When I met you, it seemed wonderful! Too good to be true! Having a person who was my *own* person, whom I had found and chosen for *myself*. You see, Mother always was terrified that I'd be kidnapped again, and if any man so much as smiled at me, she was suspicious. She'd never known a moment's peace of mind, poor darling. After Daddy died I was everything she had in the world, you know."

I knew. She snuggled closer in my arms. "Do you

remember that first day in Tom's valley? You were so grim and surly – and rather gorgeous too!" She giggled, and I thought, here we were like lovers anywhere, reminiscing. Only we weren't going to have the chance for any of it to pall, for the love to tarnish, grow old and die.

"I thought about taking you home to meet Mother, then I knew she'd spoil it for me. She'd be suspicious, make herself ill trying to find out all about you, insisting that you were after my money, making me promise."

She gave an exasperated sigh. "Poor Mother never gave me any cause for vanity, I can tell you. She never thought any man might love me for myself alone. Honestly, Greg, money can be hell, with the sort of friends it attracts. Before I met you, it seemed that Mother was right. Young men, old men, handsome, ugly men – all of them looking beyond me, their eyes glistening as they counted the Rowe fortune. With you, for the first time, I was just an ordinary girl. Do you blame me for wanting to keep it that way, even if it meant lies as well?"

"No, darling, I don't blame you, but you needed lessons in lying!"

She smiled. "I knew the kind of man you were. Stubborn and proud. You'd take one look at the money and decide quite ruthlessly that unless you could match it penny for penny, you weren't going to be some rich girl's pet.

"I was terrified you'd find out before we got married. Once I got to Scotland I was going to tell you everything. Do you remember how cross and jealous you were because I didn't want you at Lorna's that day? I was scared she'd give the show away, yet at the same time I was female enough to want to show off my husband to my only girl friend." She kissed me lightly. "Forgive me, Greg! I love you so much."

I leaned over and kissed her. "I love you, Laurel. And there's not a thing to forgive! It's like I told Vic, I wouldn't have missed any of it. I don't even care about the money.

177

It's yours, do as you please about it, I'm simply not interested. We're not going to quarrel about it. We're never going to quarrel about anything." Secretly I thought we'd be exceedingly fortunate if we ever got the chance. "I'll get another teaching job, we'll manage – we'll be happy, you just wait and see. All this will seem like a bad dream."

She fell asleep after that. I intended staying awake and looking for an opportunity to thwart Rowe by escaping. But it had been a long wearing day and the next thing I knew light was shining through the cracks in the door. Vibration of traffic passing must have wakened me and murmurs from the outside cabin indicated that our guards were alert too. I cursed myself for sleeping when I might have been devising some cunning method of escape.

There wasn't light enough to see my watch clearly. I was curious that there should be so much traffic on this normally quiet road.

Then I remembered why. This was The Day. The day that the subsidiary dam was to be opened and the flooding of the valley begun. I thought of poor Tom, waking up in the flat and thinking of his beloved home gone for ever.

A car stopped alongside. For a moment I thought a prayer had been answered and it was Wiggs. I listened. I knew that familiar voice.

It was somewhere about here that a cold icy sensation descended on me. Laurel stirred and the van chugged into life, and we slid very gently downwards.

I knew now why they hadn't shot us out of hand, and exactly why there were to be no marks of physical violence on us.

We were to be drowned. We were going out with the dinosaurs.

CHAPTER SEVEN

Suddenly the van stopped. The doors opened and the two grim silent gaolers came in. Anonymous-looking thugs must have been a Rowe speciality. Perhaps they were a sinister by-product of the firm, bred under colourless Frankenstein conditions, for the specific purpose of unidentifiability. Trying to describe them omitting bashed noses and unbeautiful ears, turned them into merely larger editions of the man in the raincoat who had followed me.

Laurel, barely awake, gave a frightened cry and my subsequent struggles were quite ineffectual in those grossly experienced hands. Seizing us like a couple of babes, they bound our arms and gagged us. Our legs remained free, not out of kindness of heart, but simply so that we could assist them by walking the remaining steps to the place appointed for execution. Laurel looked wild-eyed and frantic over the gag. I hoped the same idea hadn't occurred to her.

We were unceremoniously pushed back on to the floor of the van and the door closed. I tried to tell Laurel not to waste energy uselessly, but she was soundlessly sobbing.

I heard more murmurings outside, and that familiar voice again. Then the engine started up and by the angle at which we slid down the floor we were going down a steep incline.

There was a grind of brakes. The door opened and Hartley Rowe looked in. He was quietly triumphant, and with the little black revolver shining in his immaculate

179

white hands, he was just about the best-dressed and most expensive executioner anyone could wish for. In fact the deadly weapon he carried looked so incongruous with that silly sad-eyed face above it, that had it suddenly spurted water, I'd have laughed myself sick.

"Out you come. We'll take a little walk."

There was no sign of our charming cauliflower-eared twosome. In a way I missed them. Those Zombies were slightly less inhuman than the veneered product of evil before us.

We slithered out of the van as best we could. It was a cold raw grey morning. He marched us down the weedy road into the doomed valley, and past Tom's house which was looking more than ever like some ancient terrified beast helplessly awaiting the final slaughter.

I looked over my shoulder with some vague hope that the van could be seen from the road and someone might come to investigate it. However, Rowe had parked it well inside the small overhang on the corner of the winding road, at almost the exact spot where Laurel and I had first met. Ironically enough, it looked as if the same set would serve admirably for our farewell scene.

Even if the van had not been well hidden, I couldn't see the police bothering their heads about such small fry this day. I thought of Wiggs, harrassed and understaffed, coping with problems of protocol concerned with the Royal visit, the nightmare of congested traffic and finding sufficient car parks. Who would care about a nondescript van, or a fool of a man like Gregor MacGregor? As for Laurel Marsden-Smith, she was dead and gone, poor lass!

Rowe marched us past Tom's house and flung open the door of the barn. It was bitterly cold inside, damp and full of the smell of rotting hay. It was also nicely obscured from the road above.

As Rowe pushed us inside, he smiled grimly. "I never

leave anything to chance or forget the fact that every man has his price. Even your late highly efficient gaolers might not be incorruptible when they realised the value of the Rowe heiress." Incorruptible was an odd choice of word from him. "I always believe in seeing through the final details myself. In that way, there's no one to blame," he said earnestly. "Sorry about this, MacGregor. Believe me, I've no ill feelings for you at all." He actually sounded regretful too. "But you would interfere. You were warned. Often." He looked at his watch. "Well, better get on with it."

He gave Laurel a vicious push and she landed face downwards on the ground. Very swiftly, facing me, he knelt with the revolver lying ready at hand, then tied her ankles together with a piece of cloth. I thought of rushing him then realised how useless heroics would be. A bullet in the stomach wouldn't help Laurel much.

"You next, MacGregor. Just sit down quietly with your back to the wall there. Try anything and I shall have to seriously damage Laurel, which wouldn't be pleasant for anyone.'"

Making sure that Laurel was securely tied, he turned his attention to me. As he bent to wrap the cloth round my ankles, I kicked out viciously. It was a purely reflex action. It was also a mistake.

I saw the black object descending, tried to swing my head away and a screaming pain seared open the side of my face. Darkness rushed in and flooded the big black hole.

By the time I came round, I was trussed like a hen and Rowe was delicately dusting the knees of his trousers. When I moved, he said "Sorry about that, MacGregor. You really are an impulsive fellow, aren't you? Making me leave marks on you, that really is too bad!" He looked at us, glanced anxiously round the barn, a frown of concentration on the white clown's face. "This is not the ending I had intended, you know. Getting rid of one

181

person to look accidental is so much easier than two. Two bodies are always dangerously complicated." He raised his eyes to the rafters, speculating on their strength. "Place seems solid enough. By the time your bodies are found, I expect they'll be difficult to identify."

The final glance, then he made up his mind to go. "Can't keep our Royal visitors waiting, can I? You'll think of me, won't you, as I stand on the dam watching our illustrious visitor work the lever to flood the valley? I'll be just a rather unimportant member of the Rowe family – until the will is proved. Then, all the wealth and power I could wish for." At the door, he turned. "I really am sorry, you know. I abhor violence," he said. Polite to the end.

I thought of that beautiful house with all its treasures. Just how power-crazed can a man get!

"Sleep tight, children. Pleasant dreams!"

I saw Laurel's terrified imploring face, and turned away quickly. I'm no more cowardly than the next man, but I didn't want to see the things clearly written there. She knew what was going to happen, right down to why Rowe had used cloth instead of ropes to tie us. In water ropes would tighten and leave bruise marks. Rags would merely dissolve slowly with our drowned corpses.

Blood trickled down my battered face. It throbbed painfully and noisily, so that I couldn't distinguish the throbbing from Rowe's fading footsteps.

The sharp bang, like a car back-firing, was real enough. There was another duller sound, like an echo. Then silence. Presumably the van had got away.

For a time we were inert. Like all trapped creatures, for a while we struggled, whilst above our heads, the morning lightened. A faint patch of pewter-grey sky shone through the window. The dark overcast December morning was cold and bleak as the prospect of being permanently dunked into several feet of icy water before we were much older, gradually sank in.

The barn was still wrapped in black shadows, too dark to distinguish any means of freeing ourselves. However, using my knees in a tortuous jack-knife technique of locomotion, I did a painful exploratory journey toward the wall containing window and door.

Laurel sat watching, the shock of the last few weeks showing in the wide brilliance of terror in her eyes. At that moment my survival seemed unimportant if, by some miracle, she could escape.

Occasionally I halted my noisy progress to stop and listen.

There were faint sounds from the road far above. Cars, lorries, the sputter of motor-cycles, all madly tantalisingly recognisable. It only needed something to attract their attention.

Then there were footsteps.

Footsteps outside the barn. Faltering, then stopping.

For a moment we looked at each other. Rowe had changed his mind and come to finish us off! In a way, it would be a merciful relief. The crack of a gun then oblivion, rather than the slow rising of the icy waters, the slow terrible fight for breath.

It wasn't Rowe.

"Gregor?"

I rolled over the remaining yards to the door and banged my head hard against it. Bruised and panting, I struggled, like a man in an absurd sack-race, to stand upright and look out of the window.

On the outside of the glass, a hand moved, wiping away the grime. Again that indistinct murmur: "Gregor?"

A rescuer!

Someone had come to save us!

CHAPTER EIGHT

A hoarse whisper: "Gregor? Gregor, are you in there?"

Tom! Tom Markham, and I couldn't make a sound!

I struggled to bang my shoulder against the wall, hoping he would hear the faint noise. Then his face looked down at me.

"I'll try to get you out." Something had gone wrong with his voice. It was a rasping whisper. Suddenly he began to cough, with a sound like the rusty jerking of uncoordinated machinery.

His face disappeared. There was a long silence. Too long. I could hear his heavy breathing and wondered impatiently why the devil he didn't get a move on. Then his hand touched the window.

"It's no use, I can't lift the bar," he whispered, in that queer breathy voice. "Watched Rowe bring you here. Shot him beside the van. Tried to get in first but he saw me." He coughed again it was long and it was terrible. "Haven't much strength left, lung's gone, I think – losing a lot of blood. Behind the door – there's a hook – just about shoulder level." There was more coughing then silence.

"Can you hear, Gregor?" His face appeared at the window again. And even through the dirty barnwindow, the glaze in those eyes was unmistakeable. Tom was dying.

"I'm going – to the road – try – get help."

We heard him move slowly away. There was this hideous coughing, then silence. I thought he was dead.

We waited, and even knowing it was useless, we began to struggle again and our bonds got tighter.

I hated to think of how often Rowe had been at this game. A trickle of sunlight shone in through the window and now I saw clearly a rusty hook, just where Tom had said it was.

Leaning against the door, I stood up and tried to get the knot of the gag into it, but even standing on tiptoe, it was slightly above my head.

Laurel was trying to say something. Moving her head frantically, she indicated an old wooden box that lay half hidden by hay. I rolled across the floor. Using our shoulders and feet as levers, between us, we got it, inch by inch, over to the door. If all this sounds very quick, just a few moments, it all took the best part of half-an-hour, which isn't bad going considering that we were trussed like hens.

After several unsuccessful attempts, I got on to the box. At last getting the hook into the knot of the gag, without impaling the back of my neck at the same time, I lurched my whole body savagely forward.

I thought all my teeth had been forced back down my throat by the action. Then there was a tearing sound and my mouth, battered and bruised, was free. For a few seconds I choked, then my voice came back. Hopping to the window I began to yell for help, but who was to hear above the sounds of the traffic, no longer intermittent, now a steady stream? Who was likely to be walking along the road today, anyway?

I wondered where Tom was, if he had reached the road. There was no sign of him. Surely an old man, bleeding and coughing would be spotted by someone!

Using my teeth, I made a desperate try at unfastening Laurel's gag, but it was sheer waste of time and effort. I began yelling again.

After a while I stopped and listened. Surely, surely the traffic noises had lessened.

And from far away came another sound. The sound of hooters and something like a mighty cheer.

This was it. I looked into Laurel's terrified eyes and numbered the rest of our lives in seconds.

I turned back to the window to yell again. Then we both smelt it.

Burning! And past the window drifted faint wraiths of smoke.

Then both smoke and smell of burning intensified. We were coughing, choking and from somewhere nearby came an ominous crackle.

The faint wraiths of smoke became red tongues of fire. My God, we were going to burn to death.

I yelled again, choking, spluttering, my lungs bursting.

From heaven, it seemed, a voice answered.

"Tom? Tom Markham, where are you?" The voice belonged to Eva.

"The barn! Quick!"

"I can't see for smoke. The door! It won't open."

"Lift the bar!"

There were other voices, some fumbling, then the door flung wide and a policeman was untying our legs.

Eva, grimly and frantic looking gave a shriek of horror. "What are you doing here all tied up? Where's Tom? Is he not here?" She stumbled outside and stood looking at the burning house. "Oh, my God! He must be in there!"

Rubbing my numbed ankles, to get the circulation moving, I tottered after her.

"Tom! Tom!" we shouted. There was no answer, the house's mullioned windows were like dozens of fierce little bright red eyes, as it died proudly in the winter wind.

"Gregor! No! Don't!"

"Let me go!" And shaking Eva off, I seized a great spar of wood and rammed it against the window behind the sundial. The leaded glass shattered and a tide of heat and smoke roared out, searing my hair and eyebrows.

I heard Eva's scream and I pulled myself on to the sill.

But I never crossed into that blazing room.

Tom was there, right enough, sitting in an old broken chair. "Only fit for firewood, not worth moving," he had said when we moved him into the flat, in another far distant world.

Well, it was firewood now. The flames hungrily devoured its legs and their light touched Tom's face, as yet unscorched by fire. His arms hung limply at his sides over the chair. He looked like an old man, tired and heavy with years, dozing by the hearth in a highly technicoloured firelight.

The expression on his face astonished me. I had never seen him smiling like that, entirely happy at last.

If it hadn't been for the fact that his eyes were wide open, and there was a bloody hole in his chest, I wouldn't have known he was dead.

"Come along, sir." Two policemen led me gently away to where Eva stood transfixed with horror. She turned round to see Laurel standing beside her and gave a yelp of pure terror.

"Oh, God! I thought you were dead! Where did you come from?"

"Listen!"

There was a sound like thunder and it grew nearer every moment. Beneath us, the ground shook as it roared through the valley, devouring, consuming, obliterating . . .

We began to run up the hill and out of the valley. Some A.A. men were tinkering with the van, trying to move it up on to the road. They heard us shout and began to run too, leaving behind them the limp figure slumped over the wheel.

There was a nasty hole where half of its face had been. A blunderbuss at close range can make a sickening mess.

CHAPTER NINE

Behind us, the red eyes of Tom's house glowed no more. The fire had been put out by the waters, already there, devouring, lapping at the walls. Birds rose in clouds above our heads, screaming their terror and indignation. I thought, with ancient savage pity, of the hundreds of small creatures, trapped, as we had been, without God's gift of flight.

Safely on the road, we watched as the waters slowly covered the debris of the demolished village. Only the upper half of Tom's blackened house and the barn were visible, as though emerging from the bed of a wide river. The waters quietened, settled. By spring all trace of the valley would be oblitered as the reservoir grew slowly, steadily.

There were other cars now. Sightseers from Rowe's Vale had come to watch the last of the valley. They stood with strange excited faces witnessing the death of a small world. Then, turning away with pleasurable shivers, stationed themselves for a good view of the Royal party who would drive past this way, later in the afternoon.

In my arms, Laurel was crying. "Sorry, darling, just being feminine."

"You have a good cry!"

Eva stared at us, still unbelieving that Laurel was real. When Laurel held out her hand and said, "Thank you, Eva," she seemed a bit doubtful about taking it. The hand of a ghost, of a girl she had seen die beneath the wheels of the car that Saturday afternoon long ago.

"Thank you for getting here so nicely on time," said Laurel always remembering her manners, I noticed with grim amusement.

A familiar car hammered along the road doing eighty ground to a halt and Wiggs shot out. "Thank God, MacGregor! You're safe!" and contemplating Laurel as if she might vanish with the first strong puff of wind, he hold out his hand. "We haven't met before, but I – er – know of you. You had a lucky escape. Maybe you'd like to tell me about it when you're feeling better."

For Laurel was already swaying on her feet, and Eva, whose car was parked across the road, whispered, "She's looking awful. Shall I take her to the flat?"

"Yes, do that. I want to talk to Inspector Wiggs Darling, go with Eva."

Laurel started walking obediently towards the car, then like a sleepwalker turned, with her hands outstretched. Even now that Rowe was dead and we were safe, she was terrified to be parted again. "No. Not without you. I'll wait, thank you," she said to Eva.

"Anyone seen Markham?" asked Wiggs craning his head to the valley.

"He's dead. Down there in his house. He saw Rowe take us into the barn, killed him with that blunderbuss, by the look of his head. Then he tried to rescue us. Unfortunately for poor Tom, Rowe seems to have been quicker on the draw. Tom was too weak to do much about lifting heavy bars off doors, and was going to try to reach the road for help. He must have realised he'd never make it and set his house on fire to attract attention. Miss Black here, saw it."

Wiggs looked at the roof of Tom's house, afloat on the waters and took off his hat reverently. When he asked Eva: "How did you get here so providentially?" I wondered if he thought she was in it with Rowe.

Eva, confronted with the law, looked nervous and

189

anxious to please. "Callum – Greg's brother – sent me a letter to say that Greg had skipped off the train at York. It arrived this morning. I thought he would be at the flat." She paused and gave me a queer look. "However, when I knocked and got no reply, I found the door just opened. The lock was broken." I thought of Rowe's thugs and was glad they found it empty. "There was a note from Tom, propped up on the sideboard," Eva continued. "I read it, because I thought it might have some bearing on your disappearance. It had been written two days ago and as it indicated his intentions pretty clearly, I 'phoned the police and got out here as quick as I could."

Two days ago! That must have been immediately after his first abortive attempt to stay in the house when the buildings were demolished, the day we met him on the way to the Clinic.

A curious little string of events. If Callum hadn't been so naturally parsimonious, and indulged in the extravagance of a telegram for once, Eva would have gone to the flat yesterday morning and Tom would have been removed from the valley by force. He would not have been there to intercept Rowe, who would have escaped a messy end. Laurel and I would have died, and Tom – well, Tom would have found some other means to die. He was nothing if not determined. I realised now that he had always intended staying with his beloved house. I had been the one to be humoured along!

Laurel was clinging to my arm, grey and haggard with exhaustion. Wiggs said anxiously, "Get in the car, miss. I'll take you both home. Come on, MacGregor, you look pretty done in. Going to have a nasty shiner tomorrow, too."

I touched my face tenderly. I'd forgotten about it. Discomfort was getting to be one of the natural backgrounds of my existence, like shivering in a December morning, like a male model for an out-of-doors scene on a knitting pattern!

Then Wiggs, bless his heart, took out a hip-flask and offered a mighty swig of whisky. Passing it courteously and apologetically to Laurel, who showed no unlady-like squeamishness about strong drink, he took off his raincoat and put that much-maligned garment round my shoulders. We got in the car and Wiggs went over to take a look at the van. It was now being dragged on to the road and its occupant, mercifully covered by a blanket, hustled away into a waiting ambulance.

On the journey into Rowe's Vale, I outlined the main events since Wiggs and I had parted outside the Clinic.

"Always thought there was something odd about that telephone call you made. Then Doc Moore came in and said the 'patient' he'd appointed to keep an eye on you – " He looked at my astonished face and laughed. "Come, come, what do you take us for? You can't run a police force on the possible occurrence of coincidence, you know. Anyway, our man saw you heading over to the other wing, early that morning. Just before your telephone call, Dr. Folkes received a message that you'd been called back to Scotland unexpectedly, on personal business.

"You know we had them nicely taped. Could have prevented this, Tom's death, and your narrow escape," he said angrily, gnawing his moustache, "except that Rowe couldn't have chosen a better time. As you might imagine, the police force – both Rowe's Vale, Weschester and County – have been nicely hamstrung for the past forty-eight hours. That damned dam," he said, unaware of any humour. "Well, I hope it's worth all the trouble it's caused! What with security precautions, arrangements for the lunch, traffic diversions and the like, to say nothing of batteries of TV cameras and engineers swinging from every lamp standard – well, all I could get was one measly patrol car.

"By the time it reached the Clinic, Fellton was sailing out in his car – alone. The patrol car toured obediently. There's a pretty thorough check-up on anything, or anyone, behaving oddly immediately prior to a Royal visit, as you might imagine. However, they couldn't search every vehicle on the road and most of the cars parked in the lay-bys were innocent families out for nothing more sinister than a good place to watch the fun.

"Rowe was scheduled to receive the Royal party at ten o'clock, proceed with them and the other officials of the firm and the dam, to the opening ceremony. When he didn't turn up there was a mild panic and a pretty pickle that put us in.

"However, we smoothed the ground by pleading last-minute indisposition, dignity was regained, the TV commentator appeased with Rowe's understudy, smiles exchanged sympathetically, and *that* one got over reasonably smoothly.

"I was in a tizzy, I can tell you. Suspected he'd got wind of an impressive warrant – murder and a charge of embezzlement – and instead of being after him and incidentally, yourselves, there I was stuck bang in the middle of members of the Royal household for the next hour. Still," he frowned, "as I sat I wondered, unless someone mighty high up had talked, I didn't see how he could know about it before we did. It only came through just before the ceremony."

Murder was no surprise, but embezzlement certainly was! "He got through Laurel's fortune rather speedily, didn't he?"

"Oh, bless your heart, no! There's been talk behind hands about shady dealings in the firm before. Once, a year or two ago, we were asked to investigate. Rowe hasn't liked me much since. In fact, he would have had me transferred, except that his powers didn't extend to the police.

"Truth to tell, I was suspicious about Lady Marsden-Smith's accidental death especially as that porter's uniform business seemed very odd. But," he shrugged, "there was the devoted daughter's word. I couldn't doubt that."

We were in the heart of Rowe's Vale, bunting, flags and all. Crowds of sightseers milled across the roads to where the sleek black Royal car moved slowly down the road. As its occupants smiled and waved graciously, a great cheer arose.

Wiggs switched off the engine and leaned back in his seat. "Might as well give the crowd time to sort itself out. Where was I? Oh, yes! What really startled me and put the whole thing on to another footing was your story of the photos of the two girls. Now, the shock you got when they turned out to be pictures of buildings you handed me, seemed genuine enough." He gave me a quizzical look. "In my job, you need to assess people quickly and you'd never struck me as much of an actor! Anyway, it seemed a pointless pretence."

"It's a pity my marriage to Laurel hadn't been so charitably received," I said acidly.

Wiggs shook his head. "Ah, now, that's entirely different. Fraud, extortion and blackmail – you've no idea how often that angle's been tried before! Anyway, I noticed the envelope was old and ragged and concluded it was odd putting new pictures into it – especially since there were distinct impressions of the previous contents, which didn't match the outlines of the new ones.

"We took fingerprints and found – only one set. Not yours – we took the liberty of collecting them some time ago," he added grimly. "Strange that they weren't yours, when the photos had presumably been handled by you. Then I had a hunch – they were my own fingerprints! Which indicated that whoever put them in the envelope wore gloves. Now don't you think that's a sinister action for an innocent party?"

193

"What about Fellton?" I asked.

"When he saw Rowe hadn't turned up for the ceremony, it was only necessary to hint that Rowe had left him to face the music and he was falling over himself to give evidence, even to telling us about Rowe staging a road accident for a blackmailer years ago."

"Was that the one you talked to Rowe about, the day we went into the Registrar's?"

"It was," said Wiggs grimly. "Rowe loved to bring it up on all possible occasions – our unsolved crime, he called it. He knew damn well I suspected he had a hand in it. The man had been seen hanging round Fellton's surgery and Rowe's office, but they both had beautiful alibis."

I remembered how Rowe had enjoyed himself that day prodding poor Wiggs. The feeling I had of cat playing with mouse!

"Then the nurse who was in charge of Laurel, was only too willing to talk when she realised the game was up. Of course, she maintains that she thought the girl was Lorna Blagdon. Naturally, Fellton denies the porter business and pushing Lady Marsden-Smith off the train. However, there were dark hairs on the shoulder and in the cap of that jacket. A lab. test proves them conclusively as Fellton's. Bob, the porter, as you may remember, is completely bald.

"I expect your theory's right, that he got off the train at the next station whilst the girl gave the alarm, dashed by car to London arriving only slightly late for his meeting."

The last of the cars were dispersing and it was starting to rain. A few people waited at the bus stops, children still clutching tattered Union Jacks, with harrassed mothers looking angry and tired.

Wiggs dropped us at the flat. Eva had got there before us, and Laurel stared fascinated at the large parcels of food teeming out of Eva's outsize shopper on to the kitchen table.

Bacon and eggs sizzled on the stove and the smell of coffee and hot buttered rolls reminded us of how long it was since we had eaten. When Eva commanded "Sit down", we did so obediently.

After that Eva ran Laurel a bath and when she had gone quietly off to bed, Eva sighed about Hartley Rowe, as I knew she would.

"I can't understand it. Such a nice man, too. You've no idea how considerate he was." She shook her head, unbelieving to the end.

After she had gone I re-read Tom's letter:

"Dear Gregor – Sorry to do this after all you've done for me. Today was too much – you saw what they were doing to the houses. Twenty years ago I might have adapted but I'm too old to change now. Being away from my valley is just another kind of death. Don't grieve for me. I'm doing what I want to do, to rest peacefully with all the other dinosaurs. God bless you. Tom."

It was very quiet in the flat, amongst all those glass cases. One stuffed bird sang noiselessly, its throat feathers beautifully ruffled. Another fed soundless babies in a nest, their beaks wide open for that tantalising worm. A squirrel nibbled an acorn, head cocked on one side, listening, and a fox padded gently over a mossy bank, wicked eyes gleaming and one paw upraised. All immobolised, frozen into some long-forgotten moment of time.

Tom was dead but his possessions stayed the same, unmoved by the passing of the man who had loved them.

Only the blunderbuss was missing from behind the door.

CHAPTER TEN

Whilst the scandal of Rowe's caused panic and depression on the Stock Exchange, Fellton's arrest made black headlines in the national press. Laurel and I, with Wiggs were sole mourners when Tom's body was laid to rest in the little churchyard at Vansett Bridge.

Everything seemed like an anti-climax after that. Laurel, a thoroughly unwilling heroine, dodged the advances of the Sunday papers and press photographers, and we made our plans for going home.

News came of paintings sold at my London exhibition, but now with a wife to support, nothing spectacular enough to warrant existence without some secondary means of employment. At the prospect of a happy future, early ambitions came bubbling to the surface again, the dream of producing a painting to be proud of! Until that day I would teach – and practise, and practise again.

Laurel was delighted at the idea of living in Scotland, solemnly picturing a land of kilted men, and ladies wearing tartan sashes across their shoulders, all living on porridge, mealy puddens, and "shooting the haggis", whilst relaxing on quiet evenings at home, to the tune of the bagpipes!

She got along splendidly with Eva. So did I, since she had stopped wooing me and turned into a fine, sensible girl, who would make a grand wife for Callum.

Christmas trees sparkled in the windows of Rowe's Vale on the day Wiggs accompanied us to the station at Weschester.

He had been taken aback, like everyone else, when

196

Laurel decided, with great magnaminity, to give her entire fortune, except for her mother's personal bequests, to the firm. There was one condition – that it was re-established under a board of directors with even the humblest worker entitled to own shares.

The days of its feudal glory were over with the painting of the mural. A year ago, it was swallowed in a take-over bid. So although Rowe's Vale continues to expand and flourish and Rowe's is still the household word it was more than thirty years ago, there aren't many of its own teeth remaining behind the bite!

But I digress!

Laurel, since her abdication from the firm, had refused to be drawn into publicity of any kind. However, the people of Rowe's Vale had taken the ill-used girl to their hearts, and we had Wiggs to thank (with his usual stealth) for arranging our slick departure from the station, unassailed by wellwishers and reporters.

Laurel was so happy that day. She was in one of those infectiously radiant, rather mischievous moods, which did so much to make her seem even younger than her years.

As the train pulled out, Wiggs, his goodbyes said, added to Laurel: "I'm glad the story of Laurel Marsden-Smith had such a happy ending."

Laurel gave her silvery laugh. "So am I! It's like a fairy-tale. Except that I'm not Laurel Marsden-Smith."

Wiggs eyes bulged, as she coquettishly laid her head against my shoulder. "I'm Laurel MacGregor," she said shyly, "And have been for some time."

Wiggs chortled. The train gathered speed and we stood waving, leaning out, watching Wiggs till he vanished from the end of the platform.

Laurel sat back in her seat with a laugh. "Thank goodness that's over. Goodbye, Rowe's Vale. I thought we'd never get away! Poor old darling, he looked as if he'd have a fit when I said I wasn't Laurel Marsden-Smith, didn't you think so?" she giggled.

"I did indeed. You're a naughty girl!"

She smiled at me lovingly. How beautiful she was! With the resilience of youth, and good health, she had something else – the will to survive, which had sustained her through weeks of privation in freezing conditions, fed on drugs, conditions spelling death from pneumonia to many a stronger-seeming person, but all had left her virtually unscathed. She had already put on a few pounds and the dark-blue eyes shone with happiness.

"Do you love me, Greg?"

"Of course I do." It was a question asked with some frequency, but I was still managing to give the right answer.

She took my hand. "Will you always love me, whatever happens?"

I gave the usual affirmative reply to that, too.

For a moment she was silent, then: "Greg, would you still love me, *even* if I wasn't Laurel Marsden-Smith," she asked idly.

I kissed her gently. "Of course! There now!"

Outside the window, trees bare and black in the late afternoon, scurried swiftly past. There was a sharp flurry of snowflakes and as we ran into the dark, the world was shattered by the sudden dizzy radiance of unguarded windows, full of fairy lights.

"Greg! Greg!" Laurel shook my arm. "I'm telling you something – you aren't even listening. Wake up!"

With a jolt I came back, back from a dream of painting sunsets over the loch at home.

"I was right, you know," she said.

"Were you, darling?" I asked drowsily

She sat bolt upright, swinging round to face me. "What I told Inspector Wiggs, I mean."

"And what was that, darling?" I asked fondly, seeing

Callum's face when she walked into the croft, looking as lovely as she did this moment. Man, it was going to be a wonderful Christmas, right enough – and what a Hogmanay we'd celebrate!

She shook my arm. "I'm *not* Laurel Marsden-Smith."

"All right," I said humouring her with a loving kiss. "I know perfectly well you're not – you're Laurel MacGregor."

"Oh, stop being silly," she groaned. "Why don't you listen to me. I never *was* Laurel! There now!"

"What are you talking about?" I sounded cold.

"Don't you realise that's why I gave the Rowe fortune away? Because I had no right to it."

Even as I stared at her, about to ask if this was another little joke, something clicked into place. Painting Sir Arthur's unbeautiful countenance and concluding that his wife looked like a nice well-bred horse I had wondered where Laurel got her fragile beauty from. Then the day she told me she had starved before.

I wouldn't even put the thought into words. Frantically, I looked out of the window. Trees and poles, all interspersed by the gaiety of lighted windows were still spinning, the same world I had watched with such joy only minutes ago, but somehow hideously changed. I wasn't feeling Christmassy any more, or even happy. Somewhere inside a great knot of apprehension was growing, growing.

The horrible suspicion put itself into words.

"You're not Lorna Blagdon, are you?" I asked weakly.

"Of course not," she snorted, adding with typical feminine illogic. "Poor Lorna's dead. You know that perfectly well."

"Then don't tell me, Laurel – please!" I interrupted.

"Don't be silly, darling," she said, with a smile. "I want to tell you. I must!"

"And I don't want to know. I want to stay as we are – "

I wanted to say, but couldn't. At first, determined not to listen.

". . . So Mother had lots of trouble having this baby, she was always so delicate, they told her she must never have another. Well, her husband Sir Arthur died and after the kidnapping attempt (which Mother often hinted had Uncle Hartley's support), she was terrified both for the child and for her own ill health.

She fled to Antibes where unfortunately her little daughter took a fever and died. Mother was frantic, she knew her own time was probably short and if the Rowe fortune fell into Hartley's hands, the whole firm might collapse. Lonely and distracted, her daily walks took her past the orphanage where, longingly, she watched the nuns playing with the children. One child in particular fascinated her. She was about Laurel's age and very similar in appearance and colouring. She made enquiries found the little girl had come from a Palestinian refugee camp in Beirut. Her parents were terrorists who had been shot."

She paused, shook her head, suddenly trembling.

"Oh darling," I whispered, and she took a tight hold on my hand.

"I was that girl," she continued slowly. "Nearly six and with a very long memory, even then. I remembered my parents being led out, my mother screaming. I saw them die. And then came the hungry days when even something like an extra crust could turn everyone against you, wanting to tear you apart with hate and envy. I shall never forget it, never. Starving people, prisoners aren't noble or brave, they scream and cry and fight each other, and sometimes they lose control and go mad! I still have nightmares about being left behind on that long dusty trek to nowhere when the camp was bombed. Left to die. Then the nuns came along in a truck."

Again she paused, sighed. Then with a bitter smile: "They were kind and good, but I was one among hundreds and always hungry. When I heard that I was to be adopted by this nice lady, I screamed in terror. I clung to the nuns, sure there must be some catch in it. I could still remember my parents being led out to be shot. It took some time for my natural suspicions to be quelled, then at last, I accepted this new Mother and began to love her, and to forget the past.

"She was so good to me. We never visited England very much until I was grown up and Mother avoided any contact with Hartley Rowe. Fortunately for her he didn't particularly want to see me either. As a growing child is constantly changing and I wasn't all that like the real Laurel, Mother naturally wanted as much time as possible to elapse between visits. Luckily there are other things that give resemblance between parents and offspring, like speech, manners, gestures.

"As Mother and Hartley only met on the firm's business, he never had the slightest idea that I wasn't the Laurel who had departed to Antibes on that fatal visit. After I ran away with Lorna, the doctors told me how ill Mother was and knowing she might die at any time, I wasn't going to fail her when she most needed me. She had given me life, as surely as the parents who created me."

Small wonder the girl before me was so resilient. After that childhood, it wasn't quite so surprising that she had survived those dreadful days of semi-starvation and privation in the Clinic.

"I always meant to tell you, some time, Greg. Once Mother was dead. Until then it wasn't my secret to tell. You do understand?"

I had never known how to tell her, so happy to be my wife, that having once been an heiress might one day build an insurmountable barrier between us. We hardly knew each other as people yet, blinded by the glow of love and desire. But once that faded a little and children were added to the passing years' scenario, how I dreaded finding the spoiled petulant rich girl lurking behind the loving wife and mother. I had imagined her suppressed discontent with a teacher's pay and an artist's occasional exhibitions, remembering despite her loyalty how much of this world's goods had once been hers to command.

Misunderstanding my silence, she said: "Oh, darling, don't look so sad. Are you terribly shocked?"

"Shocked? No!"

Bewildered perhaps. For I had not expected at the outset of her story this wonderful sense of relief.

"Sad? God, no! I'm not sad. It's – it's marvellous." I laughed and took her in my arms. "Don't you see, this is the best thing that could have happened to us. The very best. This is wonderful. Wonderful!"

As I explained to her, we both knew that it was.

And is. And ever more shall be so.

Our secret. Till death do us part.